ALSO BY PHILIPPE BESSON
In the Absence of Men
Lie with Me

THE SUMMER BOY

PHILIPPE BESSON

TRANSLATED FROM THE FRENCH BY SAM TAYLOR

SCRIBNER

London · New York · Amsterdam/Antwerp · Sydney/Melbourne · Toronto · New Delhi

SCRIBNER

First published in the United States by Scribner, an imprint of Simon & Schuster LLC

This edition published in Great Britain by Scribner, an imprint of Simon & Schuster UK Ltd, 2026

Copyright © 2026 Philippe Besson
Copyright © 2024 by Éditions Julliard, Paris
English language translation copyright © 2026 by Sam Taylor
Originally published in France in 2024 by Éditions Julliard as *Un soir d'été*

1 3 5 7 9 10 8 6 4 2

Simon & Schuster UK Ltd, 1st Floor 222 Gray's Inn Road, London WC1X 8HB

Simon & Schuster Australia, Sydney Simon & Schuster India, New Delhi

www.simonandschuster.co.uk
www.simonandschuster.com.au www.simonandschuster.co.in

A CIP catalogue record for this book is available from the British Library

Trade Paperback ISBN: 978-1-3985-5605-8
eBook ISBN: 978-1-3985-5606-5
eAudio ISBN: 978-1-3985-5607-2

The authorised representative in the EEA is Simon & Schuster Netherlands BV, Herculesplein 96, 3584 AA Utrecht, Netherlands. info@simonandschuster.nl

This book is a work of fiction.
Names, characters, places and incidents are either a product of the author's imagination or are used fictitiously. Any resemblance to actual people living or dead, events or locales is entirely coincidental.

Typeset in Palatino by M Rules
Printed and Bound in the UK using 100% Renewable Electricity at CPI Group (UK) Ltd

MIX
Paper | Supporting
responsible forestry
FSC® C013604

What has become of those
slow, idle summer evenings,
stretched out to the last glimmer,
even to the giddiness of love,
to its tears, to its sobs?

—Marguerite Duras,
Summer 80

TODAY

This morning, as I turned onto a street in the city where I live now, I thought I recognized his face, his walk.

An absurd idea, of course: So many years have passed since that fateful summer that he would be greatly changed. And it would have required an unlikely combination of circumstances for me to bump into him here.

And yet, like some strange detective, I couldn't help following that figure simply because it struck me as familiar, trailing after a stranger based purely on his resemblance to the man that *he* might have become.

I found myself shoving my way through crowds on busy sidewalks, crossing roads amid the blare of car horns. I would slow down whenever he stopped, cursing the stoplights that turned green at the wrong moment, then hurrying after him again. At last, unable to bear it any longer, I sped up so I could pass him and turn to face him.

Because I needed to see. To be sure.

If you want to know the truth, I have never managed to rid myself of that story. It has never left me. It's still there, somewhere, lurking in the depths of my memory, and now and then it surfaces. In fact, this was not the first time I

3

had been suddenly drawn to a shadow, a shape, a fleeting apparition.

Nostalgia? Perhaps. A longing for our lost carefree youth. A sort of absence? Probably. As if this particular void could never be filled.

Guilt? Yes . . . The guilt of not having seen it coming.

Tell me, reader, do *you* know why the most beautiful stories must always end badly?

1985

I am eighteen, and it's summer. The beginning of summer. From the deck of the ferry that connects the mainland to the island, I look down at the rows of vehicles below me, in the belly of the ship. Some of these families, including ours, have had to wait hours before boarding. Some children running between the lines of cars catch my eye; I was one of them, not so long ago. Then my gaze lingers on the sailors who are steering the boat, their white uniforms dazzling in the sunlight. Soon they won't be needed anymore; a bridge will be built, because important people have decided so. Finally I look up at the seagulls, aloft on the wind. You would swear that they are motionless in flight.

And I close my eyes.

I breathe in the mingled scents of diesel and salt, I listen to the crash of waves against the ferry's hull, I feel the steady swaying. I don't know if I am sad or happy. Probably a bit of both. I think about the academic year that has just ended—twelve months spent cramming for exams at prep school—and I imagine the future that awaits me, in Rouen. It's far away, Rouen, far from my native Charente, and I have a feeling that nothing will ever be the same again, that my adolescence is

7

over, even if I would like to cling to it a little longer. I think about the classmates I have known since middle school or high school and whom I will no longer see as often, if at all. It's a heartbreaking feeling. Already, at such a young age, I find it unbearable to lose people. And yet I am smiling a little. Or, even if I'm not smiling, I can sense that my expression is calm. Not only because of my closed eyes. Nor because of the warm sunlight on my skin. No, this sweetness is from the knowledge that I will soon be on the island again.

When I open my eyes, there's a little boy, about six years old, standing in front of me. He's watching me—examining me—with an odd look on his face. To be more precise, it's my T-shirt that he's staring at. The T-shirt is faded, with a low neckline, emblazoned with an image of Mickey Mouse. Presumably he thinks I'm too old to be wearing a T-shirt like this. Or maybe he's a Disney fan and he imagines we might be friends. I let him observe me in silence. I don't know how to speak to children. I always feel awkward around them. I look down.

My brother wasn't with us that summer, I can't remember why. Maybe he was working at Venthenat, the plastics factory in Barbezieux, to earn some money. In July and August they would hire students to replace the workers who had gone away on vacation. Anyway, my brother has never really liked the island. I think it was the islanders that he didn't like. He couldn't understand their mentality—what he saw as their isolationism and their prejudices, even if he never phrased it like that. So this summer it's just my parents and me. They signal to me that I should head back to the car because we're approaching the wharf.

When we dock in Sablanceaux, it all comes back to me in an instant: the road with all its potholes from the thousands of tourists who drive along it, the shapes of the stone pines, the reassuring presence of the beach, the smell of seaweed at low tide. And, soon after this, the campground where I have spent so many days, and where Christian—my father's best friend, whom he met during his military service—runs a popular stall selling French fries. A little farther on, there's a square with a carousel and a pétanque court, some low dark stone walls, some houses with bottle-green shutters, a bend in the road, and we're headed to La Noue. This is where Christian lives, with his wife and two children. This is where we will stay.

When we arrive, we are greeted with hugs. There is nothing bourgeois or affected about this; it's a sincere, spontaneous expression of how much we've missed each other since last summer, how happy we are to see each other, to be together again. I am the kind of teenager who can sometimes be a little surly or rude—or so people tell me, anyway—but with them I am never that way. It's impossible.

Christian and Anne-Marie, his wife, are the only adults with whom I can show affection in this way. I keep my uncles and aunts at a distance, seeing them as little as possible, because I don't have anything in common with them. I do not subscribe to the convenient myth about the kinship of blood; I have already learned that we choose the people we love, that we should not let anyone else make that choice for us. I am not particularly interested in my parents' other friends either. When they come to our house for dinner, I barely speak to them, often getting up and leaving the table. Nobody takes offense at this, and nobody misses me when I'm gone. With Christian and Anne-Marie, things are different. Not because they've seen me grow up—this is also true for my relatives—but because I have always been happy in their company. With them, I've never been moody or bored or crabby or whatever. It's always been easy. And, with them, there is always the summer, always the sun.

François, though, is not there to welcome me. His mother explains his absence: "He's gone into town. He probably went to buy cigarettes. He thinks I don't know that he's started smoking. He thinks I'm a fool." She says *fool*, not *idiot*. Anne-Marie doesn't use words like that.

I go upstairs to leave my bag in François's room, which I will share with him during the vacation. He and I are almost exactly the same age; I'm a few weeks older. We haven't grown up together, but we've grown up in parallel. We meet up every summer and we're used to each other. He could get annoyed at having to share his room with me, but he doesn't. I notice that he's tidied up a bit, hiding the usual chaos, and he's already put my mattress on the floor at the foot of his bed. In the evenings we always talk for a long time before falling asleep, even after it's dark outside and we can hardly keep our eyes open. During the first few days, we like to catch up on each other's lives. After that, we chat about anything and everything. That's what awaits me—awaits both of us—this summer. I take comfort in the unchanging nature of these habits. After dropping my bag on the mattress, I go back down to the yard. The grown-ups are sitting around the table and Anne-Marie is serving drinks; I can see a bottle of Pernod, another of Martini Rosso. I don't hang around. I'm eager to go off in search of my friend.

I walk up Rue de la Cailletière. The sidewalk is so narrow that I am constantly brushing against the walls of houses, the hooks that hold shutters open, the branches of hollyhocks. Then Place des Tilleuls opens out in front of me. I look at the café and see François sitting on the front steps, a cigarette dangling from his lips. He is wearing his usual black tank top, jeans, and flip-flops. Beside him, standing against the wall and also smoking, is a boy I have never seen before. I approach without a word. Suddenly, sensing my presence, François looks up. Sunlight glares in his face, forcing him to squint, but despite the dazzling light, despite his half-closed eyes, he recognizes me instantly and jumps up to give me a bear hug. Unlike most boys our age, he doesn't coolly shake hands, but wraps his arms around me. (Has he caught this craze from some American TV show?) The other boy watches us, looking vaguely surprised, so François introduces us: "Philippe, Nicolas. Nicolas, Philippe." This is all he says. First names are enough, for now. We can fill in the blanks later.

Then, squeezing my shoulder and smiling with genuine pleasure at seeing me again, he asks: "When did you get here?"

We walk toward Grenettes Beach. None of us really decides this, it's more like a reflex. Our footsteps take us there on their own. It's far from being the prettiest beach on the island: the pebbles tend to put off sunbathers, and there are weeds growing on the dunes. It's mostly used by surfers, since the waves are big, but François and I have been coming here since we were kids. We have spent so many afternoons here, leaning against the split-rail fence, sheltered from the wind.

While we're walking, I ask this Nicolas kid some questions, more out of politeness than curiosity. François answers for him: He's from the mainland but he and his mother came to live in La Noue last winter; she got a job at the mayor's office, and a place to live. There's no mention of a father, so I imagine his parents must be separated, maybe divorced; you see this kind of thing more and more these days. Nicolas hardly even seems to be listening, as if we were talking about someone else. He takes a drag on his Marlboro, and the smoke curls around his lowered face. The three of us are side by side, walking in step, with François in the middle, so I'm able to observe Nicolas without his knowing. He's skinny in the way of boys who've just had a growth spurt, and his long blond hair hangs down

13

over his cheeks. His entire being radiates a sort of languor. I want the summer to darken his skin and teach him our impish nonchalance. It'll come, I tell myself. François must have chosen him for a reason.

When we get to the beach, it's packed. It's early afternoon and nobody wants to miss out on a single iota of sunshine. It's high tide too, so the kids can go swimming once they've digested their lunch. I contemplate this accumulation of colorful towels, shapeless bags, coolers and parasols, this heap of still-white or newly reddening bodies (because it's still early in the season), this mix of couples, kids, babies, and wrinklies (very few people are here on their own). It's a sight that's familiar to me.

The island has not yet become bourgeois. People come here with their caravans, their canvas tents. Nobody has a second home—second homes barely even exist, let alone the kind of villas that get full-color spreads in design magazines now. It's a place for cheap vacations. Having booked their spot under a pine tree months in advance, the tourists at the campground settle in for three or four weeks, cooking quick meals on a gas stove under the awning, eating from paper plates at a folding table, drinking aperitifs from plastic glasses in the cool of evening. Nobody bothers with fancy restaurants and everybody watches their pennies (although they don't mind paying a bit extra to treat the little ones to a waffle or an ice cream), and they all sleep in the same tent, bodies packed close like sardines. And, every afternoon, religiously, they go to the beach to lie in the sun and take a dip in the sea. The days pass without you noticing. As a child, I never noticed the days passing.

"We should have brought our trunks," says François.

I see that he's watching a girl. She's about our age, maybe a bit younger, but really pretty, with plump little breasts. She pulls at the elastic of her bikini bottoms before turning over to tan her back. Beside her are two adults who must be her parents, along with a guy of about twenty. I can tell François is wondering about who this guy is, and when he wonders something and doesn't get an answer, he asks me: "You think that's her boyfriend?"

"It could be her brother," I speculate, before adding: "Better for you if it's her brother."

He smiles, then explains: "I saw her at the market earlier."

In the mornings, François works at the market with his father, who parks his butcher van by the side of the Cours des Écoles every morning. When he was younger, he would just wrap up the meat and take the customers' money, but now that he's passed the CAP certification, he really works with his dad. Not as equals, of course, because Christian has twenty-five years of experience, so what he says goes. But gradually François is finding his feet.

"She looked right through me," he says. I can't tell if he's disappointed or relieved. Sometimes he believes that the beautiful girls of summer could never be interested in the butcher's son in his van, that they're repelled, kept at a distance. Other times, he remembers that he's good-looking, that girls' eyes are drawn to him, and that in the light, unreal atmosphere of vacations seduction comes more easily, because nothing is serious, everything inconsequential.

I whisper: "You could always talk to her tomorrow, if you see her again."

He waves my suggestion away. "Tomorrow never comes." He has learned that there is no time to lose, that tourists never stay for long, that he must seize the day or end up empty-handed.

To our surprise, Nicolas sighs impatiently and says: "You want me to go and talk to her?"

François turns to him, wide-eyed. "You'd do that? But how would you go about it?"

Nicolas shrugs. "I'd just wait until she gets up to go in the water, then I'd walk over there and say that you're into her but you don't know I'm telling her that . . . something like that, you know?"

François doesn't even bother concealing his pessimism. "Nah, forget it."

The three of us sit down, vaguely despondent, with our backs to a fence. François kicks off his flip-flops and digs his feet into the sand.

I think about his desire. It's the same desire felt by every eighteen-year-old boy since the dawn of time: the desire to make use of their brand-new body and to touch, caress, embrace, to take and then abandon a girl's body. The desire is there: obvious, visible. It doesn't hide. It has no shame. Far from covering itself up, it is eager to be seen, to be carted around like a pack of cigarettes in the pocket of your jeans, like a fanny pack on your waist, an earring dangling from your lobe. It champs at the bit, inseparable from a kind of frustration. The less it is satiated, the bigger it grows. It is at once highly focused (on girls' vaginas, their breasts) and general (almost any girl will do). It would be even more explosive if the boys knew that they would not always be eighteen, if they knew that what awaited them was a life of offices and tax returns. The desire is innocent of its future diminishment.

My desire is aimed at boys, but essentially it's identical. It is simply tinged with uncertainty because probability is not on its side, and a feeling of transgression because it is less popular, more original.

François says: "So what about you? Have you spotted a guy you like?"

We stay at the beach for quite a while, leaning against the barrier, not speaking. I can feel the sun on my face, like a balm. I pick up handfuls of sand and watch the grains trickle slowly between my fingers. I feel my muscles relaxing, as if I'm siphoning away the tension I've accumulated during these weeks of being a trained monkey: the long days in prep school hell and the restless nights in my noisy dorm, cramming my head full of superficial knowledge intended to offer the illusion of learning when the moment came, suffering test after humiliating test so I could be in the best possible shape for the national exams, the ones that would offer me a pathway to the most prestigious universities—the grandes écoles in Paris. Little by little, I let go of the stress that gnawed at me when, in vast exam rooms filled with clones, I had to swallow the shock of finding myself faced with questions on subjects I knew almost nothing about, straining to remember instead of really thinking, scrawling my answers as fast as possible so I could finish before the gong that signaled the end of the exam, never feeling satisfied afterward, then waiting for the results that would decide if my future ended here or if it went on. I breathe out the dread that took hold of me every time I passed through the door separating me from my examiners, my judges, and the anger that filled me when I failed, and the fragile hope I felt when I thought I'd done reasonably well. I wash away the residue of my pessimism and my exhaustion. After all, I succeeded in the end. I passed those damn exams. Maybe it's time to come back to the light, to tranquility.

I ask Nicolas: "Are you a student?"

Before he has time to reply, François tells him: "Oh, yeah, I forgot to say: Philippe's the brainiac of the gang. Our boy genius. He'll go far. Just ask my dad—he says it all the time: 'He'll go far, Philippe.' Which is his way of telling me that I'm a loser. Although he forgets that I passed the CAP on the first try, and that it works out for him perfectly to have me as his hired help."

I must admit that François has it bad: it's true that his father is always praising me, which is embarrassing because it's like he never had the opportunity to feel proud of his own child so he had to invest his pride in someone else's instead. I have tried to get out of it by explaining that there are far more prestigious academic paths than the one I'm on, but it makes no difference. I also thought that the revelation of my homosexuality might dampen his enthusiasm, but it really didn't. Sure, Christian is still baffled by it—it's so far from his frame of reference, a boy who likes boys. It's the kind of thing the market vendors make dirty jokes about. But in the end his admiration overcame his discomfort. He's fine as long as we don't talk about it. And I'm happy to go along with that. And when the vendors start up with their smutty innuendos, I just pretend I don't hear them.

Finally, Nicolas answers my question: "I failed my bac, so I'll have to retake the final year of high school."

I console him, even though he wasn't asking for sympathy: "Don't worry, you'll get it next time." And even as the words leave my mouth, I realize that they make me sound like a straight-A student talking down to his inferior. (I may as well have said: "People like you often have to take it twice.") My words have the same clunking sonority as a coin tossed in the plastic cup of a homeless person crouching in a doorway. Nicolas's vaguely annoyed scowl tells me I am right to suspect all this.

"So you're queer?" he says. I might easily see this abrupt change of subject as a ploy to throw that coin of condescension back in my face, but it is nothing of the kind. Nicolas simply has nothing else to say about his educational failures. It's not something he really cares about, or at least, not something he feels like discussing. He adds: "I mean, I don't care if you're queer or not, it's just that I don't think I've ever met one before."

"Well, there you go," I reply with forced levity. "Your terrible oversight has now been rectified."

He smiles back. It's the first time I've seen him smile. It lights up his whole face, emphasizing the fineness of his almost-feminine features. It also suggests that Nicolas's listlessness is not necessarily his destiny.

After that, we keep on talking about anything and everything.

I ask them if they have any plans for Bastille Day. François mentions the inevitable fireworks display at the Saint-Martin port, then pokes fun at the public dance party advertised by posters all over the island: "It'll just be a bunch of old people." We are like all boys our age: we have no desire to mix with adults. We don't listen to the same music as them. In fact, they don't really listen to music at all anymore. For us, everyone over forty is old, and we feel sure that we will never be forty. We'll be dead before then.

François talks about his Honda 100 cc, becoming annoyed as he says: "The engine's stopped working. Stupid piece of shit . . ." Not only do I know nothing about machinery, but high speeds scare me and the noise of motorcycles gets on my nerves. So I don't say anything. François turns to Nicolas, who looks totally blank, then gives up on the subject. His words are carried away on the breeze, lost among the weeds on the dune.

"What's playing at the movie theater?" I ask. (There's a cinema that opens in Saint-Martin in July and August, showing popular movies a few months after everyone else has seen them.)

François almost chokes on his incredulity. "We're not going to sit inside!"

I beat a quick retreat. "I was just asking! Like, if we've got nothing better to do one day, or if it's raining . . ."

Nicolas changes the subject again. "I like your Mickey

T-shirt." I mention the little kid on the ferry, and he says, laughing: "So you're saying I've got the mental age of a six-year-old?"

Our conversation is punctuated by long silences, during which we contemplate the beach, the sunbathers, the pretty girl, two muscular dudes throwing a Frisbee around, the pretty girl again, but almost never the sea, since nothing is happening there, and since it's always been there and always will be. There is no awkwardness to any of these silences. They're just there.

This is 1985, so there are no cell phones. We don't spend hours on end staring at screens, reading our texts and emails, constantly receiving notifications, downloading apps, playing *Pokémon GO* or *Angry Birds*, watching videos, listening to the latest hits through earbuds. We are not each in our own little digital bubble. The three of us are together. A little bored, sure, but together.

François says: "So shall we get going?"

We go to visit Christophe. He and François have been best friends since they were kids. They used to be neighbors, living in either half of a duplex on Rue du Peu Breton, before François's parents decided to "build their own place" a little farther off, on Rue des Coquelicots. They sat together in primary school, then went to middle school together. Everyone said they were inseparable, like a pair of lovebirds.

(One day, Anne-Marie secretly showed me a photograph from the family album in which the two boys were standing in front of a metal fence one winter morning, wrapped up in almost identical coats, like twins. I remember being deeply touched by that photograph. It told a story of friendship, of course, but also of something more unusual: the two boys had grown up on an island that could only be reached by boat, protected from the world beyond. As I examined the photo, I felt envious. I wished I could have been like them, been with them.)

Christophe's mother opens the door to us. "He's asleep," she says. "But I can wake him, if you want." François says we do want, and she disappears.

We go into the living room to wait for him. The three

of us sprawl on the couch, legs spread. It's an old couch, imitation leather, the edges darkened by time. On the coffee table in front of us are two magazines, one about fishing, the other about knitting. The television is like a big black cube watching us with its single eye. On top of it is a doily that Christophe's mother must have crocheted herself. On the wall is a giant jigsaw puzzle showing a French village with a church and its spire, the colors faded. I say: "Christophe's house is kind of ugly, don't you think?"

François shrugs. "It's always been like this. And I don't think it's really that ugly."

Finally, Christophe appears, still sleepy. He is surprised to see me. "I thought you weren't arriving till tomorrow."

To which François retorts: "I told you it was today, but you never listen. And you never remember anything either . . ."

I struggle to extricate myself from the couch so I can kiss him on the cheeks. He greets Nicolas too (I deduce from this that they know each other), then slumps down in an armchair. "I'm beat, guys. You fucked up my nap."

I should explain here that Christophe has to wake up at four every morning to go fishing with his father. (Fish are easier to catch very early in the morning because the light is changing and their eyes have to adapt to the variations in brightness, meaning that their vision is reduced—Christophe explained all this to me once when I asked.) After they have brought in the nets, they have to go straight to the market to sell the day's catch. So if Christophe wants to enjoy the evening, he needs to sleep through the afternoon. We know all this, but it doesn't stop us from dragging him out of bed prematurely whenever we feel like it.

"So what's up?" he says. He often says that: "What's up?" François replies: "The opposite of down."

This doesn't make Christophe laugh anymore. It did at first, but not now. He starts to grumble, so François says maybe he should stop asking stupid questions if he doesn't want to hear a stupid answer. Christophe pouts. It's so like him to fall for the same joke every time.

"So I got my driver's license," I say. "On the first try too!" (This is the first piece of news that comes to my mind. I don't tell him about the exams I took, the whole year I spent in a state of exhausted enslavement, about the one thing that has fully occupied my attention until now, maybe because I know that Christophe couldn't care less—for him, I'm just a summer friend, a vacation buddy—but also because this way he'll think: Now we won't have to ride around on mopeds or motorcycles all the time.)

I'm pretty proud of my accomplishment. The license, of course, does not only mean that I am now able to drive a car; it is a watershed moment, the crossing of a border that is no less real for being invisible. Suddenly you are no longer seen the way you were before. You are a grown-up, presumed to be responsible and independent. From our first entry into the world, we are dependent on our parents, on their decisions, their rules and permissions, their goodwill, their availability. We are molded into docile followers. And then, for the first time, we can do things for ourselves. We get in the car alone, we sit behind the wheel, we choose where we want to go. We have a power over life and death. Or something like that, anyway.

Christophe mutters: "I'm going to take mine in September, when the season's over."

How many times have I heard this expression, "when the season's over"? On the island, during summer, many of the natives work seven days a week, putting their ordinary existence on hold so that they can make a year's worth of money from the tourists. When summer is over, and calm returns to the island, they once again have time to look after their own lives, their own business.

François says dismissively: "Well, more to the point, you can't take it until you're eighteen. Speaking of, what are we doing for your birthday?"

Christophe was born on July 19. Every year, we organize a sort of party for him. Or we celebrate together, anyway. It's an important date in our calendar, a marker, an event that we wouldn't miss for anything in the world, even if we would never admit that. Christophe looks surprised. "We're going to Le Bastion, aren't we?"

Le Bastion is Saint-Martin's only nightclub, a rallying point for the town's youth—both those who come here on vacation and those who live here year-round. Some nights, that mix works well; other nights, less so. But when we're there, we always drink and smoke and yell over the sound of the music. We stagger around, and sometimes we even dance.

"You should lose a bit of weight first, don't you think?"

François suggests sharply. "You won't be able to hit the dance floor like that."

It's true that Christophe weighs about two hundred pounds (although he is pretty tall—almost five eleven, as he reminds us whenever we attack him for his weight). He hasn't slimmed down much since the last time I saw him. The word that always comes to mind to describe him is *lumbering*. Even so, I feel like François's teasing goes too far sometimes. "Stick up for yourself," I tell Christophe. "You shouldn't let him rag on you like that!"

Christophe rolls his eyes, as if to say that things have always been this way and there's no reason why they should change now.

At this precise moment, I surreptitiously glance over at Nicolas and catch a grimace on his face, as though he too is bothered by the way François bullies Christophe, or maybe the way Christophe just sits there and takes it. I could be wrong, though, and I don't know him well enough to feel comfortable asking him what he thinks.

François says: "Who wants a beer?"

I don't know how long we stay there, slumped in the living room, cans in hand. We have a remarkable capacity to do nothing. There is at least a reasonable explanation for this lethargy where Christophe and François are concerned: they get up at dawn and work hard all day. Nicolas and I have no excuse, really, unless we want to argue that we need the rest after a frantic school year. Anyway, I absolutely love our laziness. I spent the whole winter dreaming about this.

Whenever I woke up at night, in my narrow dorm bed, shivering with cold, and it took a superhuman effort to lift up the blanket; whenever I brushed my teeth or shaved in front of the cracked mirror in the communal shower room; whenever I was stuck in a classroom with all the others, with a view of the asphalt courtyard and its dead trees interrupted only by the bars on the window; whenever I struggled to force myself to eat the shapeless food in the cafeteria, amid the indescribable din of forks and knives scraping against plates; whenever I found myself speechless when faced with the convoluted questions of the teachers whose main ambition in life seemed to be to make us give up, to usher us toward the exit door since we were clearly not cut out for a grande école;

31

whenever I would have to sit for hours at my desk, facing the eggshell-painted wall, vainly trying to memorize some impossible equation; whenever I collapsed with exhaustion at two in the morning, without having the faintest idea of what was going on in the world outside . . . Yes, whenever any of this happened, I would dream of this moment, now, when we would be together again, with nothing to do, barely even speaking to each other, just drinking cans of beer, in someone's house or at L'Escale, where we would feel the warmth, where we could savor the beams of sunlight slanting through the open windows and staining the floor tiles gold, and to keep myself going I would repeat in my head, like an incantation: it'll be good. And now that it's here, I can say: yes, it is good. It was worth dreaming about.

Suddenly, I don't know why, someone starts talking about the Air India plane that disintegrated in midair a few days ago at thirty-one thousand feet above the Atlantic, off the coast of Ireland. Flight 182 was flying from Montreal to Bombay, with layovers in Toronto, London, and Delhi. More than three hundred people were killed. But what fascinates us is the passenger who booked a ticket under the name of M. Singh but never boarded the plane, while his suitcase was placed in the baggage hold and transferred during every layover until the bomb inside it exploded. François sounds almost admiring: "It's crazy, isn't it? Like something out of an action movie or a *Tintin* comic!"

Nicolas nods enthusiastically. "Can you imagine the odds against it working? Normally that suitcase wouldn't have been allowed on board. Can you imagine how that stewardess must feel, the one who agreed to let it on?"

Christophe is the only one to show any empathy. "And what about those poor people on the plane? Have you thought about the poor people who were killed?"

I don't say anything. I just fiddle with the Rubik's Cube I found wedged between the couch cushions. I'm trying to make it so that each side is all one color, but I get lost as I spin it and spin it, and I end up throwing the cube onto the table, muttering: "God, this game is stupid."

A little later, Christophe's mother pokes her head in and points out that her husband will be home soon, and it would be better for all of us if he didn't find his living room occupied by a bunch of work-shy teenagers, the air thick with cigarette smoke. "We were about to leave anyway," François says nonchalantly.

On our way out, Nicolas tells us that he's going home because if he doesn't his mother will worry herself sick. Suddenly, I see him as an obedient, considerate, well-behaved boy. (And, deep down, that's what we all are, even if we absolutely refuse to recognize the fact.) I'm afraid that François will make fun of him for this, but to my relief he doesn't react. I watch Nicolas walk away, with his skinny body and his hunched shoulders. There's something sweet and touching about him.

François stares at me: "I get the feeling you like him."

I look down. "Yeah, but not in the way you think."

We walk back along Rue des Coquelicots. When we reach the house, I can see Virginie, François's little sister, standing at the open gate with her jump rope trailing on the ground. She's thirteen. As soon as she recognizes me, she runs into my arms. She apologizes for not being here when I arrived: "I was at my friend Nathalie's house." She seems to feel she needs to justify this absence, as if she has committed some unpardonable sin. I smile at her, and she asks: "What have you been doing all afternoon?" Virginie is notoriously curious.

François glares at her. "None of your business."

She shrugs at this, then grabs my hand and drags me toward the house. "Come on, I want to show you something!" The something in question is a poster, pinned to the wall of her bedroom, of Modern Talking, a German pop group consisting of two men with silly haircuts: the dark-haired one who plays the keytar, and the blond, bovine one who sings "You're My Heart, You're My Soul," the big hit of the moment. "Aren't they gorgeous?" she gushes.

That evening, as soon as we've finished eating dinner, François and I quickly leave the table, to the loud disapproval of our respective parents, although in reality they don't need us there and are protesting for the sake of it, understanding as they do our desire to be alone together after all this time. We go up to our lair, where we immediately lie down, each on his own bed, and stare at the ceiling while we continue our rambling conversations until we finally fall asleep.

Just before his eyes close for the night, François will have time to mumble: "Say what you want, that girl on the beach is hot as hell."

34

The next day, when I'm woken by sunlight filtering through the shutters, François isn't there. He got up ages ago, to go to the "laboratory" next to the house. That's our name for the building—bare white walls, tiled floor—where the carcasses are delivered from the slaughterhouse and stored in cold rooms before being sorted, boned, cut, and trimmed, where the hunks of meat are deveined and sliced up on the wooden chopping block. It is here that beef becomes rib eye and sirloin, that pork is transformed into sausages and bacon, that lamb ends up as chops and legs, and veal as escalopes. (And when that's done, they still have to scrape the blood and guts from the chopping block, wash the knives, and sluice the floor clean.)

At the stroke of seven thirty, all the meat was transferred to their enormous butcher van, which they drove to the market in La Noue. Christian parked the juggernaut in its usual spot, greeted the early risers, then went straight to L'Escale for a drink with the other vendors. Meanwhile, François opened the van's tailgate and shelf, and wiped the refrigerated display case until it was spotless. He turned on the lamp above the work surface and added a roll of paper to the cash register before checking the knife racks and putting butcher paper and string in their allotted cubbies. He cleaned the grinder and the slicer one last time. Just to be sure, he checked that the doors to the refrigerated cabinets were securely shut, and that the waste drawer was empty. He moved without thinking, having performed these actions a hundred times. And then he waited for his father to finish his glass of red, while hoping that no customers turned up: François fears they won't take him seriously because of his age, and besides, he doesn't really know how to speak to customers. His father is a natural at that; he has the charm, the wit, the patter; people are instinctively drawn to his smile, his energy, his ribald remarks. François, so full of confidence with us, his friends, remains a little withdrawn when it comes to the rest of the world.

I go downstairs and walk through the hallway that leads to the kitchen. Not a sound. Apparently I am the only person in the house. Anne-Marie, of course, has gone to Rivedoux to open up the French fry stall at the campsite. My father has probably slipped out to buy his newspapers: he reads *Charente Libre* every day, the satirical weekly *Le Canard Enchaîné* every Wednesday, and the sports magazine *L'Équipe* from time to time, generally after a big game in Le Championnat, although there's no soccer being played in July. My mother must have gone with him to pick up her copy of this week's *Paris Match*. I can imagine them, sitting at a table in L'Escale, each with a cup of coffee. Later, my father will walk over to Christian's van and the two of them will chat whenever there's a break.

My mother, for her part, will go for a walk along the narrow, seaweed-strewn Saint-Sauveur beach; she likes it because it isn't full of tourists.

There's some coffee left in the pot, so I reheat it while trying to rouse myself from sleepiness. Through the window, the sky is electric blue. I love this morning solitude in the house. It says: the vacation has well and truly started. A summer of slow, useless, lazy silence lies ahead.

When I think about it now, it was wonderful, having nothing to do, being unproductive, simply drifting in languid inertia, with nothing to bother me, nobody to boss me around. It was wonderful that, all of a sudden, my entire existence should have no purpose, no aim in sight.

I sit for a long time at the kitchen table, elbows resting on the waxed tablecloth, the bowl between my hands, staring into space, not a thought in my head. I don't even start wondering how I'm going to fill the day. A fly lands inside a jam jar, capturing my whole attention.

At last, I get up to toss the dregs of my coffee into the sink. From there, I can see the yard: Virginie is crouching on the grass, under the cherry tree, busy doing who-knows-what. When I go out there to join her, I realize that she's dug a hole in the lawn and surrounded it with white pebbles. Now she's making a cross out of two twigs. "Whose funeral is it?" I ask. She gestures with her chin at a dead toad beside her. I look at it with interest. "Does he have a name?" She looks at me blankly. "You have to give the dead a name," I explain. "Otherwise they die twice."

She considers this. "Let's call him Sam, then."

I don't ask why. I don't know anything about the mourning rituals of little girls. (At eighteen, I have been miraculously spared an intimate knowledge of death; it won't last.) Virginie places the toad with painstaking care inside the hole, then covers it with earth. I say: "Okay, I'll leave you to it. I'm going to take a shower."

A half hour later I leave the house, abandoning Virginie to sit alone on the low stone wall around the yard; she's used to it. This is an era where children can, without fear, still be left at home unguarded, when the doors of houses are never locked because we know that nothing bad will happen.

I pop over to the market. I was right: my father is standing beside the butcher van while Christian serves his customers. When I reach the van, I call out a greeting. François asks me if I slept well. After that, we chat for a while. Obviously I'm not surprised to see him in his white apron, but all the same, in that uniform, he doesn't seem like the same person anymore. I notice a few bloodstains around his waist. I watch his fingers as he handles the meat. I can see from the look on his face that he is fully concentrated, that he is determined to do a good job, to make his father proud. No, he's not really himself. I don't hang around. "I'm going for a walk," I say. Nobody pays me any attention.

A little later, during my wanderings, I bump into Nicolas. He's sitting on the small bench under the statue of the Virgin Mary, casually kicking at the pine needles strewn all over the ground. It's an incongruous image. At first he can't see me.

He's listening to a Walkman, and the music in his ears must cut him off from the outside world. I walk closer. He finally notices me and takes off his headphones.

"What are you listening to?" I ask.

"Aznavour," he replies.

I'm a little shocked by this. "That's old people's music. And it's kind of depressing, don't you think?"

He looks a little shocked in turn. "I don't think so."

"Can I sit down?" I ask.

He nods, and we sit together on the bench without speaking. The silence isn't awkward.

After a while, we hear the pay phone near us ringing. Someone must have dialed the wrong number. We don't move. I think about François. If he could see us now, he'd probably say: "Jesus, don't you have anything better to do?"

(I know now, of course, that all this glorious inactivity was an illusion.)

The next day, as the afternoon is drawing to a close, the girl from the beach reappears.

We're at L'Escale, drinking beers. Our usual thing. And of course, when I say "we," what I mean is: François, Christophe, Nicolas, and me.

Nicolas is the first to spot her. He elbows François (gently— you don't want to make it too obvious) and four faces turn toward the girl. (François told Christophe about her the day before: he couldn't help himself, he was desperate to talk about her, as though this was some kind of erotic obsession, or— who knows—maybe something more.) All four faces turn in the same instant. The girl acts as though she hasn't noticed this (whereas, in reality, she would have to be blind not to). She sashays in wearing a flared gingham skirt that looks like something a figure skater might wear. Her sandals are golden (a detail that has stayed with me—I don't know why). She's with her parents and the twenty-year-old guy. The mother and her daughter head toward the postcard rack and spin it slowly. Some of the cards are fairly tacky, showing women's bare, tanned asses in thong bikini bottoms; others include recipes for regional dishes. The father examines the book display, a mix of the latest bestsellers, paperbacks, biographies of famous people, and political essays. The boy stands in front of the store's selection of magazines, and I have a feeling he's staring at the plastic-wrapped porn section. We try to stay cool. Christophe swallows a mouthful of beer with all the casual elegance of . . . well, a nervous teenager. Nicolas and I go back to our conversation about the Greenpeace ship that's just been sunk off of Auckland, the *Rainbow* something. Only François continues staring at the girl.

The father picks up a book and leafs through it. I recognize it as Le Clézio's *The Prospector*. He whispers to his wife: "Everyone says this is a good one."

She replies: "Well, get it, then." Before adding: "Ten postcards should be enough, right?"

He makes a face to signify his ignorance of such matters. The girl moves with astonishing grace. She's practically en pointe. Maybe she is a figure skater, after all. It's hard to imagine anyone else making those kinds of moves in a village café. The young guy calls out: "I'll wait for you outside." Apparently he's not into this sort of place. When he passes close by us, François glares at him as if he's a rival. "Maybe you should make it a bit more obvious," I suggest sarcastically.

Nicolas tries to reassure him. "Especially since he's her brother, not her boyfriend. Can't you see they look alike?"

"I'm not so sure about that," says Christophe.

Finally, the three of them stand in line to pay. Ahead of them, an old lady is buying a Loto card. While she fumbles in her purse, the storekeeper says in a loud voice: "Same numbers as usual, Mrs. Morel?"

The old woman replies: "They'll hit the jackpot one day."

A man in motorcycle leathers, holding his helmet on his hip, asks for some tobacco and OCB rolling papers. Then it's the family's turn. The father pays for everything. The storekeeper says: "Shall I put it all in the same bag?" The father doesn't understand her at first, and she has to repeat the words slowly, as if she's talking to a foreigner. The family, we realize, must be Parisians, unused to the local accent.

This revelation ought to make the girl seem vaguely contemptible—we hate "people who live in the capital"; François even calls them "the occupiers"—but somehow it seems to halo her with an even more singular aura.

We wonder what François's next move will be. Call across the room to her? Stand up abruptly and "accidentally" bump into her? Follow her and hope that she notices him? In any case, we're sure he won't let her walk away again without trying something. Instead he just sits there like a statue, hands wrapped around his pint of beer, looking wretched and defeated.

Just when he appears to have missed his opportunity, Nicolas gets up and grabs the girl's arm, as her parents head out of the door toward the sun-soaked Place des Tilleuls. What surprises me is her lack of surprise. It's almost as if she's been waiting for this to happen. Nicolas says calmly: "We're going to the Bastille Day dance in Saint-Martin tonight. Will you be there?" (He invented this lie on the spot, which throws me off completely. If anyone had asked me prior to this moment, I would have told them confidently that he had no imagination and was incapable of dishonesty.)

She looks at him, then at the three of us, sitting sheepish and silent around our table. "See you there at ten?" she says.

Nicolas nods, without the faintest trace of emotion on his face. "Ten o'clock. See you then."

And then she's gone, probably because she doesn't want her parents to grow suspicious over why she is taking so long. We just look at each other, speechless at Nicolas's audacity, and wait for François to react. Before he can, the girl comes back into the store and says: "I'm Alice, by the way."

In return, the four of us each say our name, like schoolkids taking turns to shout "Here!" during roll call. She smiles at us, then leaves again, with one last twirl of her gingham skirt. We're left wondering if we've just dreamed the whole thing.

In a shaky voice, François says: "I take back what I said about the Bastille Day dance."

There is something ridiculous and touching about the hour that precedes our departure for the dance. I watch François as he meticulously gets ready. First he shaves, very carefully. He checks in the mirror that not a single recalcitrant hair remains, then—in his obsessive quest for a smooth chin—ends up cutting himself. It's hardly even a scratch, and the bleeding stops almost immediately, but to François it is a gaping wound that will soon become an unsightly scab. "Ugh, that's all she's going to see when she looks at me!" He tries to come up with a solution. "Hey, do you think your mom might have some kind of cream or, I don't know, like, some makeup that could cover up the scar?" When I say no, I see the early signs of panic on his face. I am tempted to laugh at this, but that would only aggravate the situation. Next, he puts some gel in his hair and slicks it back. He has thick, black, silky hair, which would look better if he let it hang loose. Suddenly he looks like John Travolta in *Grease*. I mention this to him and he tells me I don't know what I'm talking about. He even adds with an uncharacteristic twist of cruelty: "Since when do you know what girls like?" I let the subject drop, even though I feel sure that I'm right. Then he splashes cologne

45

on himself, in generous quantities, and I nurture the secret hope that the smell (sandalwood) will fade before we make it to the dance. Thankfully, when it comes to clothing, he opts for a more classic approach: jeans, white T-shirt, denim jacket, white sneakers. Now he looks more like Pierre Cosso in *La Boum 2*. I make no comment: I had a crush on Pierre Cosso in *La Boum 2*.

(Looking back at this scene now, I find it incredibly moving: We were eighteen, and all we cared about was that the girl or boy we liked should like us back. Nothing else in the world mattered. As people, we were wonderfully malleable, at the mercy of our hormones, at the mercy of the moment itself. Afterward, we got older and we lost that: life sucked us into its spiral of futility.)

Next come the negotiations with the adults in our lives: we need to borrow a car and agree on what time we should be home (because our parents still try to act like parents, imposing rules and imparting to us the wisdom that we inevitably lack— and we accept this role play because we're not really rebellious, just kind of loutish). Strangely, the negotiation proves easy. Christian shrugs and says: "Just take the Kadett." The Kadett is the car that Anne-Marie uses in summer to go to Rivedoux. True, it has eighty thousand miles on the clock, it's a vaguely beige color, the paintwork is scratched, and the back door has a massive dent in it, but it goes: it will get us to Saint-Martin and back, and that's all that matters.

My father adds: "I want you back here by two in the morning at the latest!"

We're dumbstruck by this. We were expecting him to say "by midnight" in a peremptory tone, and we were already preparing to haggle like street vendors for an extra hour. His offer is beyond our wildest hopes. We promise to comply, hands on hearts (as if we were agreeing to abide by the terms of an international peace treaty): "You can count on us."

None of the adults tell us: "And whoever's driving home mustn't touch a drop of alcohol." This is 1985, when driving along country roads after three beers does not seem to alarm anyone. Times have changed.

When we get in the car, Virginie stands by the door and begs us to let her go with us. She knows we're going to say no, but she asks anyway. She asks because there are times when the loneliness of being thirteen weighs heavily on her. Too old to be babied by her extremely busy parents, who don't pay her much attention, and too young to hope to be allowed into the mysterious world of late adolescence, she is stuck in a miserable no-man's-land. But I think her begging is also a testament to her affection for me, the summer boy, the one who helps her bury dead toads. I don't say: "You're too young." I put a hand on François's thigh to prevent him from pronouncing that regrettable phrase (older brothers are sometimes deliberately mean), and instead I swear a solemn oath: "We'll bring you something back from the dance, I promise."

As we drive away, I glimpse her in the rearview mirror. It is, I confess, a somewhat heartrending image. Then she sits down on the low stone wall.

First we stop to pick up Christophe. We honk the car's horn outside his house and he appears in the doorway a few seconds later. He, too, has slicked back his hair, but only on the sides. With his chubby cheeks, this is not an ideal look. When he gets in the back seat, he laughs. "Jesus, I'd forgotten what a piece of junk this car is!"

François instantly fires back: "You want to ride your moped there instead?"

Christophe shoots me a hopeless look in the rearview mirror.

François directs me to Nicolas's house (I've never been there before). It's on Rue des Chênes, a little out of the way, in a sort of subdivision. Nicolas is waiting for us by the roadside, leaning against a power pole and smoking a cigarette. "Have you been waiting here long?" I ask.

He shrugs. "I don't know, maybe fifteen minutes?"

"But I told you we'd honk when we got here."

I wonder if he's come outside so we won't meet his mother, or because he's ashamed of the place where he lives, or just because he likes being alone.

To reach Saint-Martin, we drive along the back road, through forests of pines and tamarisks, past vines and empty fields, avoiding the potholes (back then, there was no smooth asphalt, no cycling paths: wealth had not yet reached the island, nor had environmental awareness). I place my hands at ten o'clock and two o'clock on the steering wheel, just like the instructor taught me, and, ever the good student, I follow the speed limit. (I also felt like I was responsible for the souls in the car.) It's late evening, my favorite time of day, when the sky turns pink and the heat of the day gives way to a soft warmth.

Window lowered, arm hanging out, face turned to the shore, François starts helplessly voicing all his hopes and fears. "If she agreed to meet up, that means she likes us, right? What do you think she'll be wearing? Nicolas, are you sure that blond guy is her brother?"

We try to calm him down. We all know instinctively that, when it comes to girls, the only certainty is that nothing is ever sure.

François doesn't listen to us. "I'm telling you, she likes us."

The dance takes place in the small Parc de la Barbette, which runs alongside the citadel walls at the entrance of the town. Poor Vauban, the military engineer who designed these battlements, must have imagined he was protecting the island from enemy attacks. Today his creation serves only to contain the assaults of drunken dancers. The park's lawns have been transformed into a giant open-air dance floor, its borders marked by paper lanterns. Tomorrow, the grass will be trampled, muddied, strewn with trash; it will probably take some time to recover its former luster. For now, the strings of multicolored lights are hung from posts and tree branches. The windows of the neighboring houses are decked out in French flags. Beside the makeshift dance floor there are fishermen's huts that have been turned into stalls selling waffles, pancakes, churros, cotton candy, candy apples, and ham or pâté sandwiches. There is also a bar, under constant siege, where keg beer and box wine are served in plastic cups. The dance floor is filled with people of all ages, moving around under the orders of an overly talkative DJ named Didier (he keeps repeating his own name: "Didier's next song is . . . ," "Let Didier entertain you," "Didier takes you

51

higher," "It's Didier on the decks tonight"). When we turn up, Jean-Pierre Mader has just finished singing "Macumba," and Didier starts playing "Live Is Life," the "top fifty hit" (Didier presents this as irrefutable evidence of the track's greatness) by the Austrian group Opus. "I warned you it would be shit," François points out.

Nicolas glances over at the port, where the pleasure boat masts rise into the air and the walls of the harbormaster's office are lit up. He watches a beach ball as it drifts out to sea. In a quiet voice, almost totally drowned out by the pounding music, so that we cannot be sure we've heard him correctly, he says: "Well, I think it's beautiful. I'm happy to be here."

François eyes the crowds, hoping to spot Alice among them. I am going to remind you now—since we've all forgotten, since we can no longer believe that it was ever possible—that nobody had cell phones back then, so there was no way to locate another person instantaneously; we couldn't call them to find out where they were. Random chance still existed, and with it came uncertainty, the risk of not being able to meet, even of being stood up.

And suddenly the tall blond guy is standing in front of us. A ripple of unease moves through the group. Why him? Why him, and not Alice? Could he be here to tell us she won't be coming? Or to warn us off his girlfriend? As we stand watching nervously, he leans down to Nicolas and shouts in his ear (above the chanted chorus of "Na-naa na-na-naa"): "I think you're looking for my sister."

François, having been unable to hear these words, looks questioningly at Nicolas, who yells his own name in the guy's ear, then says, "Good to meet you," before turning to us and explaining the situation. We are all relieved, but François especially, realizing as he does that there are no rivals on the horizon. He looks as though he could almost kiss this handsome stranger, or at least like he loves him already. Marc—for that is the tall guy's name—calls out: "Follow me!" And we obey without a word.

In single file, we trail him through the crowd, weaving in and out of bodies, trying not to get burned by cigarette ends or knock over the glasses of beer held at arm's length by dancers. People elbow us in the ribs and stand on our feet, and we in turn stand on other people's feet. Just when I feel as though I'm about to get swallowed by the mass, François grabs my hand and pulls me after him. Slowly, haltingly, we make our way toward the battlements. And there, at last, we see her: Alice. She is sitting on the wall, sipping what looks like Coke through a plastic straw. She hasn't seen us yet, and the fact that she's off guard makes her even more desirable.

We all kiss cheeks, as if we're old friends reunited after a year apart. It's there right away: a sense of familiarity and camaraderie. Alice makes fun of François for the gel in his hair. Unfazed, he lies: "Philippe told me to do it—he said it looked better like this." I feel a little betrayed by this, but I don't retaliate. I notice Christophe rubbing at the sides of his head to get rid of his own hair product. Nicolas smiles. He's genuinely handsome when he smiles, all the more so because the smile is spontaneous and he's obviously unaware of his own beauty. We are all happy. The air smells of sugar and salt: candy apples mingled with the sea.

Even so, we know nothing about her. Alice. So we immediately start bombarding her with questions. We learn that she is seventeen and a half (she insists on the half), that she has just finished high school, and that she will be a freshman philosophy student at Nanterre in September. She says *Nanterre* as if we're supposed to know what she's talking about, and when she says *philosophy* we all look at her like she's some sort of alien. Marc, her brother, is just one year older, and he's studying advanced math. From the way he says this, we can tell that he's not very enthusiastic about it. We are all impressed, even if we try not to show it. It's been drummed into all of us that math students are the crème de la crème. Alice and Marc live with their parents in the fourteenth arrondissement, "near Rue Daguerre," which means nothing to us. We are all from the provinces, and none of us has ever set foot in Paris. To us, it's another world: a world that doesn't interest us, or that strikes us as inaccessible without making us wish it wasn't. Their father is an executive in La Défense. Having by now realized the extent of our ignorance, Alice explains: "That's the business district. It's crazy there—a new skyscraper goes up every day! And they opened a huge mall there three years ago, Les Quatre Temps—you must have heard of that?" We have not heard of it. Alice and Marc look aghast. When they tell us that their mother is a psychologist, we're shocked. Or maybe intimidated, without really knowing why. I imagine this woman seeing her patients in a large white apartment with molding on the ceiling. There's no doubt about it: these people are not like us.

When it's our turn to talk, we keep it brief. François and Christophe just say that they work with their dads, without going into detail. Nicolas mutters that he failed his bac. I force myself to gloss over the HEC prep school I've just finished and the business school I will enter in September. Having said that, I can tell that our new friends are more interested in my CV, as if they're thinking: This kid could be one of us. I already feel like a bit of a class traitor—the one who will leave behind his modest background to join the ranks of the elite. So I emphasize my roots in Charente, because I want them to know that I'm *not* one of them.

After these introductions, you might expect our two groups to remain at a distance. After all, they're bourgeois and we're not; they're Parisians and we're not; they're just passing through and will soon be gone, while three of us will stay on the island. But that's not what happens. Despite our differences, or maybe even because of them, we seem to get along really well. The party atmosphere probably has something to do with this. I mean, who can resist Madonna's "Like a Virgin"? Who wouldn't be swept away by the magic of purple Spandex leggings, a jacket with shoulder pads, a red bandana sprouting from the back pocket of a pair of jeans, or a fanny pack, all shaking along to the same beat?

"This Didier guy's not bad, actually," François admits. "I bet we all end up thinking he's cool."

Didier's skill on the decks sends us all onto the trampled lawns, under the multicolored string lights, and makes us dance. And boy, do we dance. Nicolas, with his long, skinny body, offers a somewhat lazy hip sway, forever behind the beat, but wonderfully elegant all the same. Christophe, encumbered by his extra pounds, sweats buckets—stains spreading under his armpits, beads forming on his forehead—and yet he's the best dancer of all us boys, moving in perfect sync. François dances lasciviously, rolling his hips in mimicry of the sexual act he wants to perform with Alice. Marc shuts his eyes, as if he's possessed by the music (but can anyone really be possessed by Baltimora yodeling along to "Tarzan Boy"?). When I dance, my body is stiff as a board, and I suspect I look like a total freak. To nobody's surprise, Alice moves with a natural grace.

We also drink. A lot. We take turns going to the bar, returning with six plastic cups, held three to a hand: a perilous exercise, but we manage not to spill any of our precious alcohol, and the evening carries on like that, with us getting ever drunker and dancing ever more.

After a while, I've had so much to drink that I feel the need to relieve myself. Nicolas offers to come with me. We can't find the chemical toilets, so he says: "I've got an idea. Follow me." And we climb on top of the battlements and piss into the sea. The two of us stand there, side by side, dicks in the air, laughing as we try to send our piss as far into the Atlantic as it will go.

After we've finished, as we're preparing to climb down, I see Nicolas swaying unsteadily, about to lose his balance. I grab his arm, a little violently, I admit, since I am terrified by the idea of him falling into the sea, twenty feet below. He bursts out laughing: "You should see your face! I wouldn't have fallen, you know."

"You laugh, but it's happened before," I say grimly. "Every summer, there are idiots who mess around up here and fall onto the rocks below. Some of them get seriously hurt. Some get killed! The water's really shallow, you know . . ."

He's still laughing. "Come on, admit it—that'd be a beautiful way to die."

"Yeah, very funny," I grumble. "I think we should go back now."

Just before midnight, a rumor spreads across the dance floor, starting as a whisper and ending as a roar: the fireworks are about to start. Seconds later, there's a sound like gunfire. The racket is deafening as a series of bombs, flowers, cascades, blazes, and suns explode in the sky, sent up from two boats moored a few hundred feet off the coast. The pyrotechnics are unusually imaginative: we are treated to peonies, palm trees, chestnuts, and weeping willows. People gasp as incandescent smears stain the darkness.

Marc, standing beside me, starts giving a lecture: "Did you know that the basic principle of pyrotechnic combustion is derived from the black gunpowder that Marco Polo brought back from China?"

I roll my eyes. "Oh yeah?"

He goes on, oblivious to my boredom. "Yeah. How it works is there's an oxidizing compound, some kind of nitrate, that releases oxygen, and a reducing compound—sulfur with carbon—that serves as fuel."

I turn to face him, unsure what to make of this erudite monologue. He gazes out at the illuminations. "The explosion heats the metallic compounds to high temperatures, and that's what produces the colors."

"Is that what you learn in advanced math?" I ask.

This time, he turns to me and smiles. I find his smile disturbing. The fireworks reach their climax. Everyone is staring at the lit-up night sky and the rain of stars.

And then, after a second of silence, there's a thunder of applause. Someone says: "Wow, they really went for it this year." Someone else says: "Yeah, that was amazing." A little old lady, looking deeply moved, says: "It always has this effect on me."

François says: "Let's go back to dancing!" He has not lost sight of his objective: to seduce Alice.

Didier, who is now on fire, seems determined to help him in this quest, playing hit after hit: Jeanne Mas's "Johnny Johnny" is followed by "When the Rain Begins to Fall" by Jermaine Jackson and Pia Zadora. Even then, we can sense that the music of the 1980s will go down in history as the ultimate exemplar of tackiness, but that tackiness enchants us all the same. True, this involves an abdication of one's intelligence, but such an abdication is an essential preliminary to abandoning one's inhibitions and dancing in a sort of trance.

François tries moving closer to Alice, but she shies away from him. At first I think she doesn't want to be hunted in this way, that she would prefer to be the one in control (because I can sense a strength in her, a stubborn insistence on not being submissive). Then, I imagine that she is teasing her admirer's desire. But perhaps there is another explanation for her reticence: What if it's Nicolas she likes, rather than François? What if she's attracted to the boy who grabbed her arm in L'Escale, the one who invited her to the dance? It's true that Nicolas looks like he's in his own little world, cut off from the jostling crowd around him, and I can see how Alice might find this intriguing. Anyway, I catch her flashing him vaguely sultry looks that he, for his part, appears not to notice.

The music keeps playing, but the crowd is starting to disperse now. I can see adults heading toward the parking lot or going home on foot. Some of them are too drunk to walk straight and have to be held up by their friends. The ones left behind are younger, and Didier is playing house music now. In other words, we have moved into another dimension. I sit down in the grass, away from the crowds. Christophe, seeing this, comes and sits next to me. He is soon followed by Nicolas. The three of us form an exhausted, sweat-soaked circle. The sweet, smoky smell of churros clings to our clothes. From a distance we watch as François looks at Alice, and Alice looks at us, and Marc carries on dancing with his eyes closed. I suspect that there's trouble brewing.

Around one thirty, I stand up and signal that it's time to go home. We are obedient sons and we will keep our promise. Just before we get back to our car, my eye is caught by a stall selling stuffed animals. I go over there and buy a Kermit the Frog, which I hope will make Virginie happy, because I am determined to keep that promise too. We say goodbye to Alice and Marc in front of our Opel Kadett. We kiss cheeks again, and this time, fatigue wins out over fervor.

François says to Alice: "When will we see you again?"

The next morning, despite my lingering migraine, I decide to pay a visit to Nicolas while François is slicing up meat at the market with his father. From the looks they give me, I assume that my parents are surprised to see me leaving the house so early; no doubt they were expecting me to stay in the yard, lazing in the sun until lunchtime or perhaps spending time with Virginie (who was, by the way, very happy with her gift). They are also, I think, surprised that I should choose to walk (when I could easily borrow one of the many bicycles at the house) and that I don't mention where I'm going, but they don't say anything. The truth is that being on vacation means they can relax their usual parental vigilance, and evidently their son is now the least of their worries. Which is fine with me.

Just before I'm out of sight, though, my mother must feel a vague stab of guilt, because she calls out: "You should take a hat with you! It's supposed to get up to ninety-seven degrees this afternoon." This demonstration of maternal solicitude might well have touched me deeply if I weren't so grossed out by her suggestion: me, wear a hat?

On the way there, I pass various men, all of them shirtless, beach towels slung over their shoulders, fluorescent flip-flops on their feet, heading toward Grenettes Beach. One of them looks me up and down from behind a pair of aviator sunglasses. I am nothing to him, though. He must be thirty-five, and I am eighteen: there is a chasm between us. For him, that look is a way of marking the difference in our age, the distance between us, a form of superiority. He goes on his way, and remembering that insistent look, I turn around to watch his rolling gait for a few seconds. I smile. I like the idea that he's completely unaware that a teenage boy is ogling his ass and smiling at that very moment. He would probably punch me in the face if he knew.

As I get closer to Rue des Chênes, there are fewer people on the streets. I try to stay in the shade of the trees; my mother was right, of course. Even the hollyhocks are suffering: their pink corollas stare despairingly at the hot asphalt.

When I arrive outside his house, I hesitate, remembering how Nicolas waited outside for us the night before, and how this made me think that maybe he didn't want to show us the place where he lived (François had already told me that he'd never been inside). I decide to stay on the sidewalk and to shout out his name, hoping he will hear me. A few moments later, he appears in the doorway, his eyes still puffy with sleep. "What are you doing here?" he asks.

I can't tell him that I just happened to be passing, so I say simply: "I wanted to see you." (Yes, this is the truth. Something was urging me toward him: not desire, exactly, but rather the intuition that we would get along, that we could be close.)

He shows no hesitation. "Okay, I'm coming—just let me grab my sneakers."

We walk along the street, side by side, hands in pockets, with no particular aim in mind. (As I write this, I can see us very clearly in my memory: we're both wearing denim shorts and faded, baggy T-shirts. The image is precise. Stupidly, it makes me want to cry.)

"God, we got really fucked up last night!" Nicolas says. He isn't reveling in the memory or making it seem like some heroic exploit—that's not his style. In fact, he sounds regretful. He would rather not be hungover right now.

We make small talk for a while, until I mention what's really on my mind: "Did you get the feeling that Alice—"

He doesn't even let me finish my question. "Yeah."

So I wasn't just imagining it. "So what about you? I mean, with her, do you . . ."

He shrugs. "I don't know." But he can tell what's bothering me. "You think François would freak out if . . ."

I nod. We haven't finished a single sentence, but we understand each other perfectly.

He nimbly changes the subject. "You didn't seem to notice that Marc's interested in you though . . ."

"What? No fucking way!" I yell reflexively. He smiles, so I raise my eyebrows. He just keeps silently smiling. In a whisper (the instinctive voice of secrecy and concealment), I say: "Are you serious? I didn't see a thing." He kicks a stone with the toe of his sneaker. I'm so surprised that I keep digging. "He doesn't look queer at all . . ."

Nicolas turns to face me. "Some people think I'm queer. But anyway, you can't judge a book by its cover. I shouldn't have to tell *you* that."

"You don't look queer," I correct him. "You're just feminine—it's not the same thing. I mean that as a compliment, by the way."

He laughs. "Oh, well, as long as it's a compliment . . ."

I feel bad about calling him feminine. I should have used another word, like *delicate* or *elegant*. I worry that I've pissed him off. And I don't know how to make things better. Trying to take his mind off it, I return to the subject of Marc. "So you really think that Marc—"

Nicolas cuts in: "Do you like him?"

"I don't know," I say, flustered. "I haven't really thought about it."

Smiling again, he says: "Well, there you go. We're both in the same boat."

(At this stage of our lives, we were trapped in a fundamental contradiction: we wanted to make conquests, to have sex, and we were led by our stuttering libidos, and yet, most of the time, we were mired in uncertainty, caught in two minds, stuck in a gray zone, because we lacked the necessary determination or discernment or energy, or maybe all three, so in the end, pretty often, we preferred the company of our friends to possible romantic partners, because it was less complicated, less exhausting.)

Eventually we find ourselves wandering along a rocky path surrounded by sun-scorched fields. No houses anywhere in sight. Not a soul. Barely a breath of wind either. And silence between us. Only the sound of our sneakers scuffing up dust. Nicolas looks miles away. I watch him, then ask: "What are you thinking about?"

Still staring at his shoes, he says: "I was wondering how it went when you told people you were queer."

Unhesitatingly, I start telling him the story: "It was in high school, last year—"

"Fucking hell!" he interjects. "Doing that when you were studying for the bac takes some balls. I bet the others gave you shit about it."

"They'd already guessed," I explain. "It didn't take much courage to tell people, to be honest. I needed it afterward, though, to put up with their stupid jokes and insults."

"And this year," he says, "in prep school . . . was it the same?"

"It was more about intimidation," I reply. "People kept telling me that I didn't belong there. That I should just give up. That the business world is no place for people like me. You get the idea . . ."

"Yeah, I get the idea," he mutters.

Silence falls again. From the side, Nicolas's face is hidden by his hair. I suppose I could feel uncomfortable, having this conversation—an intimate conversation, I mean—with him. After all, I've only known him for a few days. But I don't. The simple honesty between us seems natural to me. It isn't something I sought or nurtured, and I didn't try to stifle it either; it just happened.

"Have you been with many guys?" he asks.

I spare him the details. "Only one who mattered."

Sounding wistful, or maybe even admiring, he says: "So you've been in love . . ."

"Yeah, but it's over now. His name was Thomas."

Silence again.

And then I say: "Can I tell you something?"

He turns to look at me. He says: "Yes."

"You won't make fun of me, will you?"

"No. I swear."

"I wanted to kill myself when he went away."

Strangely, his face remains impassive.

"I felt sure that we would have been happy together, all our lives. So I couldn't stand it when it ended. It seemed so unfair. Pretty dumb, right?"

"No, it's not dumb," he says. "It's beautiful."

When I go to pick up François early that afternoon, I'm amazed by how radiant he appears. I mean, he only slept three hours, then had a long hard morning of work, yet he's in the fighting shape of a bull entering the arena. And he still has enough energy to order me about. "We're going to the stall to help my mom out. Apparently everyone at the beach wants fries today." Without another word, we straddle his motorcycle and head for Rivedoux.

I hang on to him, and I'm not afraid, despite the high speed and the way the engine keeps stalling. I know I'm not in danger. When we were little kids, I remember, it was already like this: on the bumper cars at the fairground, it was François who would drive, who would bang into the other cars, and I trusted him. On the Ferris wheel, he would whoop and put his hands in the air and my terror would disappear. At spring tide, he would dive headfirst into the huge waves, dragging me with him, and I would let him do it.

The landscape we move through is familiar to me: the flat, straight roads, surrounded by tamarisks, live oaks, and maritime pines that look like they've been sculpted by the wind and the mist. This, too, reminds me of my childhood: it was exactly the same back then, nothing has changed, except that we used to ride on bicycles. I wonder why I'm feeling so nostalgic suddenly. Maybe I have a sixth sense that this blissful equilibrium is under threat.

Ten minutes later, we stop outside the French fry stall, where a long line of people are waiting. The campsite is full now, and Chez Anne-Marie is the one place where you can go at any hour of the day to grab a cold drink, an ice cream, a donut, some candy, a sandwich, a niçoise salad, or—best of all—a carton of fries, sprinkled with coarse sea salt, so generously served that they spill out over the sides.

François is ordered into the kitchen to peel potatoes, then shove them through the manual cutter. Sounds easy enough, but it's actually a tough job that requires real stamina. Nobody ever asks me to do it—they decided long ago that I wasn't up to it. So instead I go to help Anne-Marie at the checkout. I've always enjoyed this kind of thing: taking people's money, packaging up the food. As young as twelve, I was given the job of handing people back their change, and I performed it with admirable rigor. We've stuck to our roles ever since.

An hour and a half later, the lunch rush is over and we can relax for a while until early evening, when people will start coming back from the beach. François's mother lets us take off our aprons and escape to L'Ambiance, the bar opposite the campground, on the other side of the main road. This place hasn't changed either. It still has a foosball table, two pinball machines, and a bunch of arcade games, perfect for kids like us. Without needing to talk about it, we stand side by side in front of an arcade game, insert a two-franc coin, grab a controller each, and begin racing our cars. The sounds coming from the speakers make the whole thing feel more real: the roar of speeding engines, the squeal of brakes, the screech of tires.

We're deep in this tense battle when François starts talking about Alice: "We're meeting her tonight at L'Escale. Six o'clock."

I'm so taken aback by this news that I crash my car.

"Take it easy," he says, before explaining: "She came to the market this morning with her parents and her brother. I asked, and she said yes."

"Really?" I can't help saying.

He's surprised by my surprise. "Why wouldn't she say yes? We had a great time together last night, right? She's part of the gang now. Anyway, I get the feeling she likes me."

This time, I manage to avoid crashing.

"Did she say that?" I ask.

"Say what?"

"That she liked you."

He shrugs. "It's not the kind of thing you come out and say, is it?"

Maybe I was wrong, I think. Maybe she was flirting with Nicolas as a sort of diversion tactic and her secret target really is François. Seduction works in mysterious ways sometimes.

Gripping the controller to keep his car on the track, he adds: "She suggested that all of us meet up."

So maybe I wasn't wrong, I think. If she was into François, she'd have been happy to meet him alone. But if she gets the whole gang together, that means she can see Nicolas again.

Then I think: François is my best friend and I don't want him to get hurt, so maybe I should lower his expectations a little. So I mutter: "I think she likes Nicolas too . . ."

After a second's silence, François bursts out laughing. "Girls aren't interested in him! You're miles off. Girls like guys with a bit of swagger. He's kind of a wimp, don't you think?"

"No, not at all," I protest. "I guess he looks a bit fragile, but that doesn't make him a wimp."

"Listen," he says. "I like Nicolas, but he's definitely a wimp."

He sounds so scathing, and so sure of himself, that it gets on my nerves, as if I'm the one who's under attack here. (And there is something like this going on, if I'm honest: part of the reason I'm defending a weakling against a bully's slurs is that I'm projecting.) My blood's up, so I say: "Who says he's not into Alice?"

I instantly regret these words. First because I'm suggesting something that may not even be true. Next because I'm putting Nicolas in the firing line. And last, because I realize— too late—that I'm getting mixed up in something that is none of my business.

François bursts out laughing again. "Since when is he into girls?"

I'm flustered by this question. Is he saying he thinks Nicolas likes boys? Suddenly I remember what Nicolas told me this morning: "Some people think I'm queer." Is this what François is implying?

But what he says next allays my doubts: "He's a total loner, you know. He doesn't have any friends at all. If I hadn't made the first move, he wouldn't hang out with anyone on the island. And you should see his drawings—they're weird. Honestly, he lives in his own world most of the time."

And he punches the air because he's just pulled off a dazzling maneuver with his race car. This little triumph has nothing to do with what he was saying, it just happened to come at the same time, but I can't help seeing a symbolic connection between the two. François is the alpha. He has the upper hand. And he's just proved that twice over.

In this moment of victory, though, he says something embarrassing. (It's often this way with victors—they don't know when to stop, and it's their hubris that leads them into defeat.)

"Anyway, I saw her first."

I roll my eyes. "What are you, seven?"

We meet up at L'Escale that evening, as arranged. The boys get there first: François, Nicolas, Christophe, and me. We hang around outside to start with, near the carousel on Place des Tilleuls, watching a little girl desperately try to catch Mickey's tail while her mother smokes a Royal Menthol (I recognize the packet because my own mom used to smoke them) and offers vague encouragement. François and Nicolas keep glancing warily at each other, and I realize that this new tension between them is probably my fault. I decide to make small talk with Christophe, who doesn't seem to have noticed that anything's wrong.

"How was fishing this morning?"

"We got lucky!" he says enthusiastically. "We put our nets in the perfect place and the currents helped us out too, so we ended up catching loads of sea bass and sole, enough to keep us going for days."

Nobody is really listening to him, but we have to talk about something while we wait for Alice's eagerly anticipated (or much dreaded) appearance.

She finally turns up about ten minutes later. Our summer girl is wearing denim overalls, and we all think she looks great. Marc comes up behind her, and I notice that he's dressed in beige shorts and a tight white T-shirt that shows off his pecs. Nicolas flashes me a brief smile of complicity when he catches me staring.

We go inside the café and sit at one of the tables near the glass doors. From there, we have a perfect view of the tourists coming back from the Saint-Sauveur beach, carrying their parasols and coolers. Not far from us, a couple of boys, about twelve or thirteen, are playing pinball. I observe their glaring eyes, their snarling mouths, the way they jerk their hips as they watch the ball, the frantic movements of their fingers on the side buttons, and the loudly expressed anger when the machine flashes a tilt warning. François looks at them too and smiles.

We chat briefly about last night's dance, as if we can still hear the pounding beats echoing in the distance, then Alice changes the subject: "We went to the movie theater this afternoon. It was way too hot for the beach, and we didn't want to get burned. How long is this heat wave supposed to last?"

"What did you see?" I ask, sounding curious. (Curiosity is another good diversion tactic.)

"*Subway*," she replies. "You know, the new Luc Besson movie? Hey, I've just realized he's got the same last name as you—are you related?"

I shake my head, sorry to disappoint her.

"It's heartbreaking," she goes on. "You should totally go and see it. There's this brilliant scene where Adjani turns up at a dinner party with her hair in a Mohawk, looking miserable as hell, and her husband tells her to smile, and she says: 'When I smile I want to throw up. Is that what you want?' And over dinner she rips the prefect's wife to shreds, then finally stands up and pulls the tablecloth off the table and everything goes crashing onto the floor! It was amazing—I'd love to do that."

"And the soundtrack is crazy," adds Marc. "I can't get that 'It's Only Mystery' song out of my head."

François feigns interest. "We should go see it."

Amused by this astonishing act of hypocrisy (love was obviously making him lose it), I say: "I thought you thought it was boring, going to the movie theater in summer?"

He pulls a face. "I never said that!"

I no longer know what to make of his attempts to seduce Alice. In a way they're touching, but they're also pathetic.

We talk about loads of things after that, hopping randomly from one subject to another. People keep interrupting, so nobody ever finishes what they were saying, and sometimes we end up shouting just to be heard. We laugh loudly and our chairs make squealing sounds on the tiled floor when we move them around. It's chaotic and joyful at the same time.

We get onto the subject of politics and someone says: "Mitterrand's going to get wiped out in this election."

"We'll all be able to vote for the first time next year," I point out. "Can you believe it?"

"I don't care," says Christophe sulkily. "I'm not going to vote."

Then we talk about SOS Racisme and the big concert that took place a month ago in Place de la Concorde, and Alice says: "We were there. It was a moment of real communion, you know?" She looks so serious and profound when she says this, and François imitates her, which makes me want to laugh. I mean, obviously it's a worthy cause, but the idea that a concert can do anything to change racism just seems puerile to me—I'm already disillusioned, at eighteen.

Then the conversation skips all over the place, from Jean-Paul Kauffmann and Michel Seurat, the hostages in Lebanon, their identities already indistinguishable from their situation, to university and the grandes écoles, from the price of Walkmans ("It's scary") and beer ("It's bullshit") to loads of other things that I've forgotten.

While this is going on, Nicolas is the quietest among us. He barely says a word as he sits there slumped in his chair, legs spread and arms crossed, and I remember what François said about him being a total loner. Alice keeps looking at him and smiling, and occasionally he smiles back, but most of the time he doesn't. Marc stares at me two or three times, and I find it pleasant and a little disturbing. François does his alpha thing—he's undeniably charismatic, and I love that about him, but there are times when he seems to take up too much space. I would savor this moment more fully if I could only be sure it would last.

And then, at the end, Christophe surprises us all. The conversation has come full circle to fishing again, and we're all going on about what a romantic job it is, going out on the open sea at dawn and all that, and he suddenly gets annoyed and says: "Oh, give me a break! It's a really boring, repetitive job. Look at my dad: he's forty, but anyone would think he was sixty, and he doesn't know how he's going to make it through the next twenty years. Honestly, if I could do something else, I would, but I don't have a choice."

We're all a bit disappointed that Christophe has destroyed this myth, but it's Nicolas's reply that makes us frown.

"Of course you have a choice," he says. "Just leave. What could be simpler?"

"Oh yeah?" says Christophe. "And where would I go? What would I do?"

This seems like common sense to us, but Nicolas is not convinced. As if reciting an aphorism, he declares: "You don't leave to go somewhere or to do something. You just leave, that's it."

François cuts the argument short: "Who wants another beer?"

I meet up with Nicolas the next morning. He was the one who suggested it when we said goodbye the night before. (I am still awed by the way summer can bring these new friendships into sudden bloom, the way you can know nothing about the other person one minute and they can occupy all your hours and your thoughts the next, the way you can go from being strangers to being inseparable in the space of a single day.)

As I did yesterday, I stand on the road outside his house and call his name. I imagine we're going to walk the nearby paths again or maybe sit with our backs to a split-rail fence, the way I do with François. But to my surprise, Nicolas invites me inside. I hesitate for a moment before opening the gate, walking the ten feet or so to the front door, and entering the house. What I discover is a small, modest dwelling, intended for only two people. On the first floor there's a main room that serves as a kitchen, living room, and dining room. It has beige tiles on the floor, easy to look after, and sun-faded wallpaper on the walls. In the center there's a table covered with a waxed tablecloth and some plastic chairs, the kind that people might keep on a balcony. Overall there's very little furniture, and I realize that they must have been short of time and money when they moved to the island. We don't stay here long because Nicolas leads me straight upstairs. His mother's bedroom is on one side, next to a bathroom, and his bedroom is on the other. That's where we go. The window is open, letting in the light and heat of the day. On the walls there's a poster of Téléphone (which makes my heart ache a little when I see it because they were my former lover Thomas's favorite band) and a print of that famous photograph of Rimbaud taken by Étienne Carjat, in which the seventeen-year-old poet appears at first glance like a kid at first communion, an ordinary obedient child, but then you look more closely at his eyes and you can see the blaze to come. We sit on the unmade bed, cross-legged, facing each other. With someone else, I might sense an ambiguity in this close proximity, but with Nicolas there's nothing to worry about. Besides, he gives me a prosaic explanation for what we're doing here in a voice that sounds sincere: "It's too hot to go for a walk, don't you think?"

"Isn't your mother home?" I ask.

"No, she has to work this month," he says. "She'll get her vacation in August. She works at the mayor's office, but François probably told you that already . . ."

I nod, and he goes on:

"She got that job through a friend when we had to leave Poitiers."

"You lived in Poitiers?" I ask, surprised.

"I was born and raised there," he says. "It's the kind of city that makes you want to shoot yourself, to be honest, but you don't get to choose, do you?"

Although I fear what the answer will be, I still ask the inevitable question: "Why did you leave?"

"My parents got divorced and it didn't go well. We needed to keep our distance."

"Keep your distance from what?" I ask. I know I'm intruding, but I can sense that this is what he wants. He didn't choose to bring me to his room only because it's hot outside: he wants, maybe even needs, to talk, probably because he hardly ever talks to anyone and I—this stranger with whom he's grown close—am the ideal confidant.

Again, he doesn't beat around the bush. "My dad's a possessive guy, and he took it very badly when they split up. He can't stand it when things or people get away from him."

I continue to question him coolly and shamelessly. "Possessive?"

He's clear and curt in his response. "He can be violent too."

(I don't ask for any details about the violence. I don't dare. Did this man beat his wife? His son? Both of them? Already, though, I feel compelled to imagine it, and so I picture slaps, punches, wounds. I can also hear the father's voice— raised, sarcastic, bullying, insulting—and I don't know which is worse, the physical or the verbal violence. I glance briefly at the open window, because I need the light, the air. I don't know that one day I will write about all this, under the influence of another young man—one who looks like him.)

"One morning," he continues, "when I woke up, I realized that my mother had packed our suitcases. She told me: 'We're leaving.' And we left. She couldn't live in the same city as him anymore."

To conceal my feelings, I stick to the simple facts. "So you don't see him at all now?"

"In the end, he found out where we were, and he regularly threatens to come here. As yet, he hasn't gone through with his threats. For us, it's like being on vacation."

Throughout his confession, he has expressed himself in a neutral, unemotional tone, as if the passing of time has allowed him to view these events with a certain detachment. And yet I don't entirely believe that. I suspect that he's speaking in a monotone to conceal his own feelings. Even that last sentence—"For us, it's like being on vacation"— obliquely suggests his bitterness, his anger, his fear.

I don't want a silence to fall after this. I don't want Nicolas to think that I'm feeling sorry for him, because I've already gathered that he is disgusted by overly earnest expressions of emotion. But a silence falls anyway. I can't think what to say. I'm eighteen years old, I have no repartee. I don't know how to handle new, embarrassing situations. But Nicolas just accepts the silence. He makes no attempt to break it.

Since we are not talking, I take the time to really look at him, to observe his fine blond hair, his pale greenish-blue eyes, his diaphanous skin—the sun seems to have left no mark on him—and then I smile. He smiles back. Suddenly there's a sweetness between us. But, once again, there's nothing ambiguous about this sweetness: it's just sweetness, pure and simple. And incredibly refreshing.

I change the subject. "François says you like to draw . . ."

He waves this away. "Oh, that's nothing. They're just quick pencil sketches, you know?"

"Can I see them?"

Reluctantly he gets up and rummages under the bed, finally pulling out a green and black portfolio overflowing with sheets of Canson paper. He hands it to me, then looks away as I open it. I start examining his sketches. I don't know much about art, but his lines seem very assured, simply drawn but capturing the essential nature of each subject. He's copied a few Edward Hopper paintings (I know nothing about Edward Hopper at this point; it's Nicolas who tells me: "He's the painter of melancholy"), including one of a woman in profile, her hair tied in a bun, sitting on a bed, her arms around her knees, and another of a woman seated alone at a café table, wearing a cloche hat. I'm struck by the sadness that emanates from these drawings, and I find it hard to believe that it's all the fault of Edward Hopper and his famous melancholy.

There's also a portrait of a severe-looking man with a mis-shapen face, his mouth open. I frown at it. "Is that inspired by a painter too?"

"No. That's my father."

I remember what François said about Nicolas and his "weird" drawings.

At four o'clock exactly, we all meet up at Grenettes Beach. We spread our towels on the sand. We don't have a parasol—they're just for old people and babies. All the same, Alice did think to bring some sunscreen and she rubs it over her arms, her shoulders, her neck, her belly, and we watch her, with vague admiration, as if we were attending a show, the sensuality of her gestures making us breathe a little harder. When she's finished, she asks us if we'd like some and we all say yes, bravely but not recklessly.

She's wearing the same bikini she wore on the first day, the one that caught François's eye. In a way, it's because of that bikini that we're all lying beside her on the burning sand now, looking out to sea. In order: Marc, me, Nicolas, Alice, François, Christophe. Nobody officially decided this order, but it does, when you think about it, obey an implacable logic. Christophe at one end—he's the least demanding of all of us, the least self-important—lying next to François, his best friend. Alice between her two suitors, although that may not be an accurate description, because while François definitely wants her, nobody really knows what Nicolas wants. I'm stretched out beside Nicolas, the complicity between us

87

obvious to everyone. And then, on my other side, there's Marc and that whole unspoken attraction thing.

Our bodies, almost naked, also say something about us, of course. Christophe's is flabby and he has scratches and red marks on his forearms. François's is firm and muscular, with a line of dark hairs running from his navel down to his Speedo. Alice has skin like gold silk and her body is remarkably well proportioned, her breasts like a pair of apricots. Nicolas's body is skinny, almost emaciated, his skin very pale and dotted with moles. Mine is of no great interest, not especially beautiful or ugly, just an ordinary eighteen-year-old body. And then there's Marc, who has a swimmer's body: healthy and reassuringly well-balanced.

Even our swimsuits define us, so accurately that it's kind of scary. Christophe wears a pair of long trunks, too tight around the thighs, with big blue flowers printed on them. Swim briefs for François, alerting everyone to the generosity of his natural endowment. A classic flower-pattern bikini for Alice. A pair of khaki shorts for Nicolas, as if he just grabbed the first thing he found to hand. I'm wearing long, shapeless trunks too, allowing me to expose as little as possible. And Marc's in short trunks that show off his muscular thighs.

It's not long before François is itching to get in the water. I know him: he's afraid of getting sunburned, and swimming is the best way of escaping the furnace heat, but he also wants to show Alice what an athletic swimmer he is. If it were just us boys, he'd go straight in without hesitating, but he knows he should wait for Alice's signal. It's like when you've been invited to dinner at someone else's house and you wait for the hostess to pick up her fork before you start to eat. Thankfully it doesn't take her long to get to her feet. François immediately runs across the sand and dives into the waves, and a few seconds later we all follow him in. He starts frantically doing the crawl, heading out to sea. He must think that, here in the water, he will finally be able to show his capabilities, his ease in his own body. He must imagine that Alice will be impressed by his energy, his hot-blooded masculinity. And I must admit that the sea is his element. I have never lusted after him, because we've been friends since we were children, but I can almost feel myself aroused by the sleek power of his body.

In the water, we rediscover all our primal reflexes. We make waves with our arms to splash one another. Christophe jumps me and tries to drag me underwater—and succeeds. François does a handstand on the seafloor, only his feet poking up above the water's surface. Alice floats on her back for a while, before her brother flips her over like a pancake. I climb onto François's shoulders and wave at the crowds like the queen of England, turning my hand slowly and robotically. Only Nicolas remains aloof from these childish games.

And yet not all of this is childish. Not everything is innocent when bodies rub up against each other. Perhaps the people watching us from the shore think our tomfoolery is like a dance or some kind of mating ritual. And, if so, they're not wrong.

By the time we return to our towels, almost an hour later,

we are shivering and laughing, so exhausted that we stretch out without even bothering to dry ourselves. We love the salty drops that bead on our skin, keeping us cool. Nicolas's hair is plastered to his cheeks. At first, nobody speaks: we just rest, relax, doze. But every time we turn our heads, casually, wearily, we find ourselves looking into someone's face and a fire is rekindled. François stares at Alice's body while she lies there with her eyes closed. She appears astonished, or maybe captivated, by the whiteness of Nicolas's skin. Marc and I open our eyes at the same time and our forearms touch. In this false immobility, desire stirs. Anxiety too, at times. Like when I fear that Nicolas has sunk into a coma, or I catch sight of François scowling because Alice is ignoring him, or I wonder if I might be wrong about Marc's true feelings.

Around us, the chirping of children and the raised voices of mothers ordering them to stay away from the water. The puffing and panting of people in their thirties playing an improvised game of volleyball on the sand. Incomprehensible snatches of conversation carried on the wind. The cries of a donut vendor walking along the beach. The shrieking of seagulls and the roar of the waves. This muffled cacophony forms the soundtrack of another sweltering afternoon.

After a while, Christophe says: "This is perfect, isn't it?"

François answers for all of us: "Yeah, it really is."

Thinking about those words again now, those simple words, they weren't an exaggeration. They were just true. It *was* perfect. There was the sunlight and the salt on our skin. We were optimistic, cheerful, enthusiastic. We were carefree and lazy. We were going with the flow, surrendering to the moment. And we were together.

(None of us knew what was about to happen, of course. We didn't have the faintest idea.)

That day, though, after we've all gone our separate ways, as François and I are walking back toward Rue des Coquelicots, back to the house, I sense that he's upset about something. Irritated. Tormented, even.

"You were right," he mutters. And that's all he says.

"About what?" I ask, although obviously I know what has put him in a bad mood.

He's silent for a while, and I understand that he's finding it hard to say the words. Finally he spits them out: "She prefers Nicolas."

My instinct is to soften the blow for my friend, even if it means going against my own conviction. "You don't know that. She hasn't said anything either way, and they're not seeing each other, outside of the group. Nicolas would have told me. Nothing's happened between them."

"He's the one she likes, I'm telling you," he says, dismissing my objections. "You saw it for yourself. She 'adores'"—and here he made quotation marks with his fingers—"his khaki shorts and the moles on his back."

I think about how much I like them too, but I keep that to myself.

"I don't even exist for her."

I try once again to sweeten his bitterness. "You can't say that. She's spending loads of time with all of us, and when we were in the sea she was messing around with you too."

But his mind is made up. "Whatever. She doesn't want to be with me, period."

I understand his rancor. It's the resentment of the boy who can usually get any girl he wants, who never loses, the boy who's attractive and knows it, who is used to desire being followed by satisfaction. His pride is wounded, and the pride of an eighteen-year-old boy can be enormous. But it's not just that. After all, he could easily switch his attentions to some other girl and forget about Alice. Besides, he's smart enough to know that, even if something had happened between them, it would never have amounted to anything more than a summer romance, a fling. No, the truth is that he has feelings for her: it's maybe the first time this has happened to him, and he's as shocked by it as anyone. Even if it would kill him to admit it, he's hooked.

Still scowling, he grumbles: "What does she even see in

him? Did you check out his body? He's thin as a rake, white as a sheet, and silent as a corpse. Well, screw him and his fucking moles!" And he gives the finger to an imaginary version of Nicolas.

I jump to the defense of the accused again. "Don't be a jerk. He's your friend, remember?"

"I barely even know him," he says, and I can tell he must be really angry if he's lying to himself about this. "He only turned up here last winter. I'd never seen him before that."

I refuse to let this go. "Just because it's recent doesn't mean it's not real. You like him, you know you do. You wouldn't have introduced him to me otherwise."

"I felt sorry for him, that's all."

I smile. "Okay, I think we both know that's not true."

He looks down, aware that he can't argue with this. Not that he gives up altogether. "What I mean is, he was going through a tough time, so obviously I felt sympathetic toward him."

"Yeah, you're a regular guardian angel," I joke.

Another scowl. "You can laugh, but you know it's true: this is a shitty way to pay me back!"

Somewhat sententiously, I tell him: "You shouldn't expect to be paid back when you help someone. Virtue is its own reward."

"Only you could come up with crap like that!" he says.

(He genuinely believes this, by the way. François thinks that nothing in life is given for free, that anyone for whom he does a favor owes him one in return, that being a friend ought to be rewarded. He grew up with those principles. Not to mention that he regards me as a smug, intellectual bastard who's always moralizing, and what I've just said is the perfect illustration of that.)

We arrive at the house. Our parents are sitting in the living room, watching TV. The latest stage of the Tour de France, from Toulouse to Luz Ardiden, has just ended and the men are talking about it.

My father: "Hinault had a nightmare today."

Christian: "Hardly surprising, is it? He's got bronchitis, and the fog in the Pyrenees can't have helped!"

My father: "Well, he got away with it. Greg LeMond could easily have taken the yellow jersey off him."

Christian: "That Yank bastard would have done it too, if Tapie hadn't reminded him that he's just a domestique and his job is to help the team leader win."

My father: "I still reckon LeMond is the stronger rider. I bet you anything he wins the Tour next year."

"An American winning the Tour de France? Kill me now."

François rolls his eyes and says: "Come on, let's go to the bedroom." There, he throws himself onto the bed, arms outstretched. He's still obsessing over Nicolas: "Of course, he's got that tortured artist thing going on, hasn't he, with all his sad, dark drawings. Whereas I just cut up meat. I can't compete with that."

It's hard to contradict him on this point. Indeed, it's something that I already realized for myself: François is generally considered, first and foremost, the butcher's apprentice, the butcher's son, the boy who sticks his hands into animal innards, who slices up flesh, who gets the blood off his hands by wiping them on his apron, the boy with a job that makes girls look down their noses at him, or even wince, and on top of that he's working-class, uneducated, and not shy about expressing his views—the kind of proletarian who moans about the government and taxes, who goes dancing on a Saturday night—and this tends to provoke condescension and occasionally outright contempt from certain people. And I can't exclude the possibility that Alice, who has grown up in the fourteenth arrondissement, whose parents are cultured and wealthy, also feels somewhat disdainful toward François, for this very reason. Of course, she's not like that on purpose and she may not even be aware that she feels that way. But if this is true, wouldn't it just make it worse?

"You're wrong," I tell him.

"I'm not wrong, and you know it."

At four thirty in the morning, I hear François slipping out of the bedroom to join his father in the lab. I would like to tell him to stay with me a little longer, although I don't really know why. But I'm too drowsy to say anything, and I fall back asleep almost instantly. It's Virginie who finally drags me out of bed around ten o'clock. She gazes up at me with pleading puppy-dog eyes and says: "Don't you want to come and help me find shellfish?" Maybe I look doubtful, because she tries to convince me by adding: "I know all the best places."

I don't have anything better to do this morning and I feel guilty about the way I've neglected Virginie since arriving on the island, so I summon enough energy to feign enthusiasm and say: "Absolutely! I'm your man." (A curious expression, which I have never used before. I don't even consider myself a man. Indeed, I'm not a man: I'm too weak, too immature, too desperate to hold back time, to cling to my adolescence. But I guess the age difference between Virginie and me explains this incongruous phrase.)

While we stroll toward her secret spot, she promises me we're going to find shrimp, mussels, crabs, and periwinkles, and I listen to her endless chatter without really believing a word of it. Finally she leads me close to an old casemate that's being slowly devoured by the sea. (Nobody was talking, back then, about beaches disappearing through erosion, or at least I don't remember anyone talking about it.) You can still reach the fortified gun turret easily enough at low tide, though. We take off our flip-flops and put on rubber boots, and Virginie goes ahead of me, carrying a small net and a bucket. I've got a basket and a knife. The first things we find are some tiny crabs, just floating there in a rock pool. After that, though, we have to start searching under rocks, and it's slim pickings. Even so, Virginie's enthusiasm doesn't waver. She points out a spot covered with loose stones and I find a bunch of mussels there. They all go into our bucket.

We see an old man, who encourages us to keep looking. His face is like a topographic map, his deep, wide wrinkles like a series of rivers and their tributaries. (Years later, I will use this face to invent a character in a book.) Virginie redoubles her efforts.

I realize then that I would love it if she were my little sister. All I have is a big brother who never talks to me, who lives his own life in his own little bubble far from me, and some cousins with whom I have almost nothing in common. I can already sense (I have mentioned this before, but the memory of this particular morning reminds me once again of this phenomenon) that I am going to spend my life inventing proximities, attachments, and affections to substitute for the family ties I lack.

While we're bent over the damp sand, scratching and digging together, she asks casually: "Are you going to sleep with Marc?"

I try not to show the surprise I feel at the discovery that *she knows about me*, and that she is obviously well-informed about our summer friends. I just raise my eyebrows. With disarming sincerity, she explains: "I heard you and François talking the other night. The walls in our house are pretty thin, you know, and anyway I'm not stupid. I do understand things."

"I don't know," I mumble.

"Is he handsome?" she asks.

I hesitate, then say: "Yeah, he's not bad. The others will probably tell you that he's drop-dead gorgeous, but I'm not sure how much that matters to me."

She looks surprised. "So what does matter to you?"

I don't know how to answer this. In the end I start stammering: "Um, it's hard to say . . . Like, the feeling you get from someone . . . Their aura, you know . . . It's not just about physical appearance . . ."

"Sure, but you don't need to be in love with him to have sex, right?"

I stare at her. How does a thirteen-year-old girl know stuff like this? And should I really be talking like this with someone so young?

Unfazed, Virginie goes on: "I'm pretty sure my brother won't get to sleep with Alice, though. He's not her type at all. Still, it's probably a good thing—it'll teach him a lesson."

I don't see any point in responding to this. Not that she cares what I think. She seems pretty sure of herself.

"But I don't think she'll sleep with Nicolas either. I know Nicolas—he's come to the house several times. It's not his thing, anyone can see that."

"You think?"

"Yeah, he's too sad, and too much of a loner. I get the feeling that he's sort of broken inside."

I think about what little girls see, and how we don't see things in exactly the same way. I think about what they understand, and how we sometimes misinterpret it. I also think about how perceptive and mature they seem, and that scares me.

"I'm not in love with anyone," she says. "It's too complicated."

I don't give her the classic line: "You will be one day—it happens to everyone." I'm afraid she'll tell me that I sound like an old man. Nor do I tell her that nobody has a heart of stone, because I don't want her to think that I'm some hopeless romantic.

In the end all I say is: "Why do you think it's complicated?"

My question seems to surprise her. "Honestly? Well, first, people often mix up having sex with being in love, right. But even if we assume that love is a good thing . . . To start with, you spend your time wondering if you love the other person, or if they love you. Then, once you've got a boyfriend, you spend your time wondering if it's going to last or not. And when it does last, you end up getting bored, but you don't have the energy to start again with someone new. On the whole, I prefer dead toads."

I think about how thirteen-year-old girls are more precocious and less sentimental than eighteen-year-old boys. And that maybe they're right about everything.

"Look, crabs!" she says suddenly, and she rushes after the poor little creatures, which are frantically scuttling away to escape their pursuer.

We stay on that stretch of empty beach for quite a long time, in the shadow of the casemate. Virginie does a little dance on the pebbles, then uses a stick to draw shapes in the sand, although I can't tell what they're supposed to be. Out of nowhere she has become a child again, innocent, carefree, detached from the world and all its cares.

We head home on the path across the dunes. Virginie skims the tops of the weeds with her fingertips and kicks up sand with her feet.

A few hours later, when he learns that I spent part of the morning with his sister, François gets annoyed. "And what kind of crap did she tell you this time?"

The next day, I have a date with Marc. Apparently he spent the morning at the market, pacing around the butcher van, then sitting on a nearby bench and pretending to look through a leaflet that someone had left there, before finally going back to the van and asking François—"if you don't mind"—to pass on a message to me. (It's François who tells me all this, adding with his usual tact: "You should have seen him, it was painful to watch. He's such a fucking girl.")

The message was: "Do you want to meet up?" When I heard that, I immediately remembered Virginie asking me: "Do you want to sleep with Marc?" I figured that, if I met up with him, at least I'd know the answer to that question.

When I walk through the door of L'Escale at three o'clock precisely, he's already there. He's ordered a pint of beer and he's drunk more than half of it. He doesn't see me at first: he's staring through the glass doors at the hordes of passing tourists. Then I realize that he's not seeing any of that, he's just staring into space, lost in thought. Which means that I can observe him without fear of being spotted. It's true that he's handsome. He doesn't look like Thomas, not at

103

all: Thomas had a mop of dark hair that came down almost to his shoulders, and he was skinny, whereas Marc is blond and well-built. But I've realized by now that it's pointless constantly chasing the mirage in my memory, and that the best way of getting over it is to embrace new, unknown bodies. So they may as well be drop-dead gorgeous.

As I'm walking toward him, I think: Maybe I should come straight out and tell him that I know why we're here, and that there's no point being shy and uncomfortable and making small talk when we could just cut to the chase. But I suspect I don't have the balls or the confidence to get away with it. Besides, I kind of like those hesitant, awkward, stupid moments that come before the confession, the sudden shift of gear. (And there's also the fact that I'm still not used to the idea of a casual fling.)

Everything goes the way I expected it to. Marc politely thanks me for agreeing to meet him. In a low voice, he says: "I wasn't sure you'd come—it must have seemed weird, getting that message."

I don't say anything, because if I did, I would have to tell him the truth: "No, it didn't seem weird at all, because Nicolas guessed that you were into me, so I was just waiting for you to make the first move."

He goes on: "It's just that every time we meet up, there are lots of other people around, so we haven't really had time to get to know each other."

I feel like saying: "Yeah, right. Listen, it's obvious you just want to get me naked, and honestly I don't have a problem with that." But I remain silent and let him struggle through this on his own.

"Actually I've been meaning to ask you . . . ," he begins, and I smirk because he sounds like a guy in his fifties, before answering his questions about what I'm going to study at university. He then tells me about his own studies, repeating that he feels out of place there, and I sense that he's not talking about the subject matter. After that, the conversation moves on to the Île de Ré (he's excited by the plan to build a bridge, and since I don't want to make him feel bad, I don't tell him that the bridge will mark the end of my childhood) and tennis (he's nationally ranked, whereas I don't play any sports at all). To be honest, I'm only half listening. Most of my focus is on examining him in greater detail. He tries really hard to come across as confident, but from time to time his fidgeting hands and his fluttering eyelids betray his nervousness, his fear. I like how gauche he seems.

I'm being a smart-ass, but the truth is I'm just as keyed up about this encounter as he is. I'm simply better at controlling myself, restricting myself to a few nods and lots of *oh yeah*s.

And then, after a while, it happens: he shifts gears. I couldn't say with any certainty what it was that convinced him—maybe he saw the *yes* in my eyes or sensed the desire in my tensed body. Whatever it was, he suddenly says: "Do you want to come and see the house where we're staying?"

I accept the invitation without haggling, and the two of us immediately stand up. He pays the check by tossing a few coins onto the Formica table, without even bothering to wave the waiter over, since he's in such a rush to get out of there.

On the way, he mentions that his parents and his sister are at the beach. So the coast is clear—we will have the house to ourselves. I wonder what excuse he came up with to get out of what is the main activity for every tourist on the island. Did he tell them it was too hot, or that there'd be too many people? Did he say he'd meet them there later? And did his parents believe this nonsense? Alice wouldn't have been fooled, that was for sure. Maybe she was even in on it? Yes, of course she was. He must have told her that he was attracted to me, and she must have said: "Go for it." Maybe even: "I'll make sure they don't go back to the house for as long as you need—you can count on me." That would be very Alice.

It's an old house, not one of those chic villas that will spring up everywhere once the island becomes a paradise for the privileged (sorry, I'm rambling again). Inside, there's a gray tiled floor, thick whitewashed walls, a long oak table. I imagine it must once have belonged to some elderly locals but now it is rented out in summer by their heirs, who live elsewhere, far from the island where they grew up. I spot a veranda at the back of the house, and a small garden with a stone pine in the middle.

"I know it's kind of dark in here," says Marc apologetically, "but it's perfect for a vacation."

I hear this throwaway remark as an example of the social contempt that François feels aimed at him, although I'm sure Marc is oblivious to this subtext.

"I like this kind of house," I protest. (Do I sense, somehow, that they are doomed to be transformed, to disappear? Or am I trying to make Marc understand that he and I do not belong to the same world?)

"Shall we go upstairs?" he says.

I follow him.

Once we're in the bedroom, we get straight to it. We kiss, pressing our bodies together, stroking each other's skin, reaching for each other's erections. We take off our Bermudas and our T-shirts and we make out. His body is more powerful than I thought, and it unnerves me at first because I prefer the more gentle type. But I soon get used to it. I realize that his roughness is the consequence of a lack of experience. Not that I've been with loads of men, but I learned some moves with Thomas and I have a certain intelligence when it comes to the other guy's desires. We both come. I remember very clearly how he spurted across his hard, tanned stomach.

Afterward we lie side by side, naked on the rumpled sheets, staring up at the ceiling beams, not speaking. And in that silence, in that frozen closeness—much more than when we were going at it, a few minutes before—I suddenly realize that I could feel something for this boy. Let's call it tenderness.

I imagine François saying: "God, you're such a pussy!"

I meet up with François later that afternoon and we decide to go to Christophe's house. He should be done with his nap by now, we think. When we get there, we find Nicolas already with him. Christophe, sensing the tension in the air, hastily explains: "We bumped into each other when I was coming back from fishing and he was jogging on the beach, so I told him to drop by this afternoon."

I stare with astonishment at Nicolas. "You jog?"

"Yeah, sometimes," he says with a shrug. "Early in the morning, when there's no one around."

"It doesn't seem to be making much difference," François sneers, looking pointedly at Nicolas's unathletic body.

For once, Nicolas strikes back: "Some people like the way I look . . ."

I don't want the two of them to start arguing—I would prefer us all to return to our old chilled-out time-wasting—so I say sarcastically: "Oh, I didn't realize we were going to a cockfight . . ."

That defuses the tension instantly. It's like we all agree that it's way cooler to laze around, drinking beer after beer, talking nonsense.

To my amazement, it's Nicolas who initiates the conversation. "Did you hear about those seven high school kids in New Jersey?"

Christophe looks lost. "Where?"

"New Jersey," Nicolas repeats. "In the United States, you know?"

"Ah," says Christophe, putting down his can of Kronenbourg.

Then Nicolas starts telling the story: "These guys are all under eighteen and they're obsessed with their computers. Like, they spend hours on them, day and night, and finally they manage to hack into the Pentagon's computers! Apparently they stole the codes needed to move satellites!"

"Seriously?" I say. "It's like *War Games* or something." (We all saw that movie last winter and dreamed of being Matthew Broderick.)

Nicolas smiles. "Well, yeah, except they didn't start World War Three . . ."

It's hard to tell whether he's relieved or disappointed by this.

"What'll happen to them?" asks François.

Nicolas shrugs. "No idea. I just know that the cops arrested them. They've been accused of theft or something. Crazy, isn't it?"

"Totally," someone says, and we all nod.

I stare at Nicolas, wondering what's actually going on inside his head. Every time I talk with him, I discover a new aspect of his personality. In a way, of course, that's perfectly normal, since I met him less than a week ago. But some people are open books: you grasp their character right away and they can never surprise you. Some people show you their whole life all at once, like a child throwing his toys on the floor. Other people are like a glass brick, with no cracks or rough edges. But not Nicolas. With him, everything emerges in fragments, in snatches. And despite this, despite all these little confessions, he remains mysterious at heart. Nebulous. Only his friendship is clear and unblemished.

One subject leads to another and we end up talking about Christophe's birthday party, which will take place tomorrow. It's a chance for us to reminisce about his previous birthdays, as if, at eighteen, we're already getting nostalgic for the good old days. We remember when he was eight: his parents gave him a cowboy outfit and we had fun with his cap gun for days, as if nothing else mattered. Or his fourteenth birthday: at nightfall we all went to the casemate on Conche Beach so we could cover it with graffiti. We'd just discovered spray-paint cans and stencils, and we thought we were graffiti artists. Christophe used to tell anyone who would listen that the future was punk or something—I assume he must have seen a TV documentary about it. Or his sixteenth: we took his father's boat—again at nightfall—and sailed out to sea, without telling his dad, obviously. There was nothing new about this experience for Christophe, except that this time he was the ship's captain, and it was a starry night and we all got wasted. Last year, we spent the night at Le Bastion, and now we're getting ready to do the same thing again. Why?

Because nightclubs are where you go when you're our age, and we have no reason not to do the things that people our age are supposed to do.

"Dude, you turn eighteen tomorrow," François says. "Are you ready to become a man?"

Christophe frowns skeptically, unconvinced that this passage into official adulthood will change his life. He has understood that no great metamorphosis is going to take place. But then he smiles: he's glad he was born in the summer, during the holidays, that his birthday is a marker in all our lives, a night we look forward to.

We decide to eat dinner at the Crêperie des Tilleuls before going to Le Bastion. François says he'll pay for all of us and we shout him down: "Everyone can pay for their own meal."

François hisses between his teeth: "I said I'm paying. Now, don't piss me off by arguing about it."

Realizing that he means it, we quickly back down. "Okay, okay."

So it'll be eleven o'clock by the time we hit Le Bastion. I choose this moment to divulge the information that I've been keeping to myself: Marc and Alice will be there. Three faces turn to stare at me, and I explain that I saw Marc earlier today. I don't mention the fact that we sucked each other off in the bedroom of the house that his parents are renting. Not that I'm ashamed, I just have a feeling it would be better to keep this little episode secret for now. All the same, I do glimpse a little smirk on François's face, an expression that means: "You're not getting away with it that easily—you'd better tell me what happened!" I pretend I haven't noticed this and continue with my explanation: "And he told me they were going there tomorrow night, so I said: 'Hey, that's a coincidence, we'll be there too.'" (This is total crap, of course: I invited him to meet us there. Call it the collateral effects of the idiotic tenderness that I'm starting to feel for the tall blond tennis player.)

I don't let slip the other news that Marc shared with me: that Alice "has a massive crush on Nicolas and she's planning to go in for the kill, so it's perfect timing that he'll be there tomorrow night."

"I don't know about the rest of you," says François, "but I have a feeling we're never going to forget this birthday."

It is July 19—Christophe's birthday—and the humidity is as oppressive as ever, with thunderstorms forecast for the evening. This is good news, I think: the rain will break the heat and we'll be able to breathe again.

In the morning I drop by the market to say hi to François, who has yet again managed to sneak out of the bedroom a few hours earlier without my noticing. Seeing me, Christian comes out of the van and kisses me on the cheek, asking if I slept well, if there's anything I need. And, without warning, he slips a hundred-franc bill into my hand. He's trying to be discreet, but he's trying so hard that everyone around notices what he's doing. He winks and says: "Now you can have fun tonight."

I protest—it's too much money and I haven't done anything to deserve it—and, just like his son, he gets annoyed. So I shove the bill in my pocket (my principles have their limits), and François shoots me a look that says he's not that insistent or affectionate or generous with his own son.

After that, I go to Nicolas's house, but when I yell his name from the street, he doesn't appear. I take a deep breath, then knock at the door. Still no response. I try the latch—

the door is open. After hesitating for a few seconds, I go inside. (Thinking back to this now, it's not like me at all, this boldness. Was I just being curious, or did I somehow sense that there was something here to be discovered, a mystery to be solved?) On the table there are the remains of someone's breakfast, a cup of coffee (presumably his mother's) and a half-drunk bowl of hot chocolate. I call out Nicolas's name again. Still nothing. I go upstairs to his bedroom. The bed is unmade, but there's still no sign of my new friend. I'm about to leave when I spot his portfolio. Unable to resist, I open it. The portrait of his father has been angrily crossed out. On another sheet of Canson paper, Nicolas has sketched the Saint-Martin battlements, with the sea in the distance (the same sea we pissed in at the Bastille Day dance). I leave his room and then the house, vaguely troubled but incapable of putting my finger on the source of my unease.

A little later, I kill some time at the newspaper store. I look through the selection of books there before spotting a really short one that I've heard of before but have never read, so I buy it. It's *Bonjour Tristesse*. (One of my French teachers told me it was "lighthearted and amusing." When I eventually read it, I will discover a terrible tragedy, and I will realize that tragedies can unfold under a "lighthearted and amusing" exterior.)

On my way out, I bump into Christophe. He's wearing waders and fishing boots. I wish him a happy birthday and he asks me what I'm up to.

"Nothing much," I say. "I was thinking of going to Saint-

Sauveur and sitting on that little bench so I can read for a while. You know, where we used to go when we were kids and we didn't want anyone to find us?"

I spend the rest of my time thinking about Marc. I want to see him again, to taste his mouth and feel the strength of his arms, the softness of the skin of his cock.

Looking back, I can see how vacuous that day was. As if time had been suspended. The lull before the storm.

That night, as planned, we meet at the crêperie. When we arrive, there's already a warm ambience in there: a dozen people are sitting around a long table, all of them talking loudly, even shouting, raising their bowls of cider, flirting, gently ribbing each other, and laughing. In contrast, sitting in our little corner, we look like a bunch of quiet schoolkids. We toast Christophe's eighteenth birthday but we don't urge him to give a speech. He would hate that, and we wouldn't be able to hear his words anyway over the din at the next table.

After a while, someone mentions Alice—I don't remember who or why—and the mere utterance of her name provokes a brief exchange of looks between François and Nicolas. An awkward silence ensues.

Later, the whole room suddenly falls silent. We're so surprised, after the constant racket from the big table, that we listen in. A woman is talking about a disaster that happened in Italy around noon that day—she "heard it on the news." We gather that two dams burst in the Dolomites—a big tourist destination at this time of year—after several days of torrential rain had flooded the river. A huge mudslide crashed through the valley, destroying everything in its path. "At least sixty people have died, and they said on the news that it could be much more than that. And then there are all the ruined houses, the uprooted trees . . ." The others around the table nod sadly. "Apparently it all happened in twenty seconds," the woman adds. "Twenty seconds—can you imagine?" The others look even more stricken.

Then one of the men raises his glass and says: "Well, we shouldn't let it ruin our night. Who wants more cider?"

There's a roar of agreement, and I think about those twenty seconds that changed everything, destroyed everything.

At half past ten exactly, we leave the crêperie. The air outside is wonderfully balmy. Place des Tilleuls is full of people: couples, families, some kids our age gathered around a backfiring motorcycle, even some old people. It's as if nobody wants to go home, as if they all want to stay out and savor this perfect temperature. (Ever since then, I have sought out balmy summer evenings—there is nothing like them to soothe the soul.)

We head back to the house. François and Nicolas smoke cigarettes as they walk side by side in silence. Christophe and I hang behind. Rue de la Cailletière is strangely quiet. The hollyhocks shine in the light from streetlamps.

After promising our parents that we will be good boys ("You can trust us," we say, provoking some incredulous looks) and saying good night, we all get in the Opel Kadett and drive to Saint-Martin. We're no longer thinking about the people in the crêperie or the disaster in Italy; all our thoughts are focused on the mirror ball above the dance floor at Le Bastion, and the hundred francs in my pocket, and Alice and Marc waiting for us.

I turn on the radio and am thrilled to hear the Étienne Daho electronic hit "Tombé pour la France." François sings at the top of his voice: "When the devil of dance takes over my body, I go crazy."

There are only a few people on the dance floor when we get there, but it is still pretty early. The townies stand to one side, and the Parisians (the term *bobo* has not yet been invented) to the other. The T-shirts with pictures of Johnny Hallyday or blue-eyed wolves on them do not mingle with the Lacoste polo shirts; the faded Bermudas go nowhere near the chinos; the flip-flops stay away from the loafers; the faces weathered by sea spray do not turn to those reddened by sunburn.

We walk in, a little nervous, as if we don't belong. And it's true that in July and August the natives are outnumbered by the tourists. Thankfully, François holds his head high, and his confidence spreads to the rest of us. He must have some kind of radar, because he spots Alice and Marc instantly and we make our way toward them. Strangely, I feel like there's an awkward tension in the air when they see us, but I'm probably imagining it. Alice looks at François and says with a sarcastic smile: "I'm glad you're not wearing so much gel this time."

He chooses to smile through his humiliation, before mumbling: "You smell nice."

"Opium," she says, looking flattered, "by Yves Saint Laurent."

The rest of us make no comment. We go to the bar and order our first drinks.

We stand for a while on the terrace that leads to the battlements. The air is still warm, but a wind is blowing in from the sea. I remember the forecast of thunderstorms, but I don't want to be a killjoy so I don't say anything. In the end, though, we go back inside.

Nicolas and I are the last ones to leave the terrace and we are trying to keep the others in sight so we don't lose them when suddenly Nicolas stops dead in his tracks. I stumble into him and get annoyed: "What the hell are you doing?"

"Sorry," he mutters. He could get annoyed with me for getting annoyed, but he doesn't. He just apologizes. And I find that disconcerting. That's when I notice that his expression has changed. He looks upset, or maybe scared.

"Are you okay?" I ask.

He doesn't answer.

"Hey, has something happened?" I insist.

He waves away my concern. "No, it's okay, I just saw a guy I wasn't expecting to see. It's this jerk from my high school, and I really don't want to bump into him." I think I can discern a mix of fear and anger in his voice, which makes me want to ask him for more details. But before I can say anything, he says: "We should get going, or the others will wonder where we are." I follow him, all the while looking around, wondering which guy could have caused him to react like that.

By midnight, the place is jammed. We're one solid mass of raised arms and sweat-drenched hair, and the atmosphere is electric. We forget our historical surroundings and are swept away by the rhythm of the tracks selected by a half-drunk DJ, by the initial effects of too much alcohol. We dance until exhaustion.

I barely even recognize Christophe, who is wiggling his hips to Les Rita Mitsouko's "Marcia Baïla" while lip-syncing to the lyrics, or François, who is spinning around, banging into anyone who gets too close. I stare at Marc and smile idiotically as I sway to the music.

Eventually we move away from the others, the two of us, shoulder to shoulder. We don't dare kiss—boys don't kiss each other at Le Bastion, unless they want to get beaten up—but my skin brushes his. We're at that inane stage of new love.

I spot Nicolas standing with Alice, out on the terrace. He's smoking and she's drinking through a straw. "They saw each other this morning," Marc confides.

I'm so startled I don't say anything. He must think I haven't heard him, so he yells the words into my ears, as through the speakers Catherine Ringer sings: "Death is like an impossible thing."

"I heard you the first time!" I yell back at him. "But how?"

"She decided she couldn't wait," he says, "so she turned up at his house and they went for a walk."

Which explains why the house was empty when I got there, I think.

I want to know more. "So what happened?"

"She told him how she feels."

"And?" I prompt him impatiently.

"He said he was touched, and he thought she was really pretty, but his life was a bit of a mess at the moment, he had personal stuff to deal with, and he didn't think it was a good idea to start a relationship. So she said: 'It wouldn't be a relationship—we're on vacation, we're allowed to just have fun.' But it made no difference. Honestly, he's kind of a pain, your friend. Why couldn't he just go for it? I mean, look at us. We didn't make a big song and dance out of it."

I know I should focus on this unexpected news—Nicolas and Alice's abortive affair—but my attention snags on a different detail. "What does that mean, 'personal stuff to deal with'?"

Marc shrugs. "How should I know? Sounds like a bullshit excuse to me." Then he points at his sister and says: "As you can see, though, she's not giving up."

"She'll scare him if she carries on like that," I say. "He's kind of fragile, Nicolas. She'd be better off with François. At least she knows he likes her."

Marc laughs. "Yeah, she knows he's got the hots for her, but it's always like that, isn't it? You want the one you can't have."

I gaze out at the dance floor. Christophe is drinking another Blue Lagoon; Nicolas is walking away from Alice, out toward the battlements, and she's coming back into the club with a face like thunder. François welcomes her with open arms as the DJ plays "You're My Heart, You're My Soul" and I think how happy Virginie would be if she were here. Finally, Marc grabs my hand and shoulders his way through the dancing hordes toward the restrooms.

When we come back out, the song is ending. We just had time to kiss before being kicked out by some guys who'd gone in there to empty their bladders and started hammering on the stall door because it had been locked for too long. Spotting us together, François comes over and makes fun of our blissful smiles. Then, abruptly, he turns to the dance floor and asks a stupid question: "Any idea where Nicolas went?"

A second later, he dives into the crowd, a plastic cup held above his head like a trophy, and starts dancing again as if his question needed no answer.

But I could hear it echoing strangely inside my head: *Any idea where Nicolas went?*

Right away, I have a bad feeling.

Right away.

I ditch Marc, who seems baffled that I should care so much about anyone other than him, and go off in search of Nicolas. I wander all over the dance floor, hoping to spot a skinny boy with long blond hair. How many of them can there be? None, it turns out. I have to shove and elbow my way through the mass of bodies to reach the terrace. But when I get there, still no sign of Nicolas. Just then, lightning illuminates the sky and rain suddenly starts pouring down. It's a typical summer storm, hot and heavy, appearing out of nowhere. Immediately, everyone runs back inside the club, almost in a panic, screaming and laughing. When the terrace has completely emptied out, I have to face reality: Nicolas isn't here. I glance over at the battlements, sinister in the flickering darkness. The idea crosses my mind that he might have fallen into the sea, but I quickly dismiss it. I go back inside, completely soaked, dripping a trail of rainwater behind me. The dance floor is packed and I have to jump up and down to try to catch a glimpse of a blond head. My efforts are in vain, though, and some guy yells at me for standing on his foot. I spot Christophe, who looks out of his head, and François, staggering with exhaustion, both of them blithely unaware of the tragedy that might be unfolding. I walk across the dance floor one more time, searching its center and then around the edges. I go to the bar, to the DJ booth, to the patio doors, to the row of couches, bumping into drunken partygoers, passing the speakers that blast my eardrums, even searching every stall in the men's room: still nothing. I'm seized by a vague panic, which I try to calm down through reason. Alice, seeing the look on my face, asks me what's wrong. I lie, telling her "everything's fine," before continuing my quest, my futile quest. Around two in the morning, the dance floor clears and people start leaving the club en masse. Finally, I have to admit the truth: Nicolas is no longer with us.

When I tell the others this, they don't seem as worried as I feel. "He must be somewhere," says Marc. "Are you sure he didn't go out for a piss? Beer will do that to you."

I want to believe them, but a small inner voice keeps whispering that they're wrong, that Nicolas really has disappeared. It gets on my nerves, this voice, but it won't shut up.

Outside, the rain has stopped and the other clubbers are quietly drifting away. Soon afterward the club's doors are closed. The last employees toss enormous trash bags into dumpsters, the bouncer goes home, and silence falls. The others were expecting to find him out here, and even though nobody mentions his absence, it's all we can see: a yawning chasm in the night. We decide to walk toward the port. We stand in front of the boats as their masts make that stupid jingling sound and we wait, because you never know. But still our friend doesn't appear. We start to look at each other weirdly.

"Should we tell the cops?" I ask.

"What? God, no!" says François angrily.

I choose to ignore this. "The gendarmerie is closed at night, but if we dial seventeen, someone will pick up."

"Yeah, there should be someone on duty, at least in La Rochelle," Alice agrees.

I point at a phone box. "Has anyone got change?"

Christophe is sitting on a mooring post, half-asleep, indifferent to our conversation. As for Marc, he is just hanging back, as though he doesn't have an opinion on any of this. Or maybe he doesn't want to disagree with his sister but he also doesn't want to agree with me because my anxiety is making him jealous, so the simplest thing is just to stay silent.

François shakes his head wearily. "You do realize he's probably just gone home?"

"Without saying goodbye?" I say. "Without telling us?"

"What are you, his mother?" he replies sarcastically. "He's a big boy, he can do what he wants."

"So you think he walked back? It's a long way!"

François isn't convinced by this. "He's always walking. He even goes running on the beach. You really think he's going to be scared of a five-mile walk?"

I have to admit that François is talking sense. As I'm

starting to waver, he hammers home his advantage: "Besides, he did the same thing to me last month."

"What do you mean?"

François tells the story: "We were hanging out at Le Domalin one Saturday night, just after his exams. Christophe was there too . . . although, given the state he's in right now, he's not going to be able to back me up . . . But anyway, the three of us were there together, and then Nicolas just slips away! The next morning, he came to the market to tell me that he hadn't felt good and he'd decided to go home. He said he hoped we didn't freak out, and I told him we didn't."

I can feel the relief all around me. Of course he went home! He's a total loner, after all, Nicolas, a man of mystery. That must be what's happened. Yeah, it must be.

Except that the little voice keeps bothering me. "Okay, why don't we drive around to his house now? Maybe his bedroom light will be on . . ."

This is too much for François. "For fuck's sake, do you want to marry him or what?"—a remark that earns me a cold glare from Marc.

Disdainfully, François concludes: "Just call his mother tomorrow morning and you'll see that I was right all along."

I look around at my friends, observing the tiredness on their faces, the sweat stains on their shirts, the boozy smell of their breath. I notice that the strap of Alice's dress has slipped off her shoulder, that François's shirt is unbuttoned, revealing the hairs on his chest. My gaze lingers on Marc, and I stare into his blue eyes, trying to draw some reassurance from them.

I scan our surroundings—the empty terraces, the metal rolldown shutters covering the storefronts, the simple wooden shutters covering house windows, the glow of streetlamps, the pavement glistening after the rain, the silhouette of the harbormaster's office in the distance, the dark sea—and it occurs to me that summer is not really summer anymore, this late at night.

"All right," says François, "so where did we park the car?"

The next morning, at eight exactly, my sleep is disturbed by a harsh, repetitive noise. Since I haven't slept enough, since I've slept badly, since I drank too much last night, I'm unable to identify this noise—I just know that it's whistling in my ears without managing to rouse me from my semi-comatose state. And suddenly this unpleasant sound is aggravated by a convulsive, jolting sensation. It takes me a few seconds to realize that someone is shaking me. I open my eyes, but the light coming from the hallway forces me to close them and shield them with my forearm, as if from some violent attack. Finally, I open them again and recognize Virginie. She's speaking to me. I can tell that words are emerging from her mouth but can't make sense of them. I ask her to repeat herself, more slowly, and this time I understand what she's saying, and what she's saying reawakens an anxiety deep within me. "Nicolas's mother is on the phone. I had to answer it since there's nobody else here as usual. She wants to talk to you."

I jump out of bed, totally naked, and I don't even think about putting on a pair of boxer shorts or about the thirteen-year-old girl standing in the bedroom, I just rush into the living room, where I find the receiver lying neatly on the small round table beside the telephone in its olive-green velvet cover. Already I guess that I'm not going to like what I'm about to hear. I also guess that I might have to think of something appropriate to say, and at my age it's hard to find the right words because I don't speak that language, the language of adults or of people whose job it is to deal calmly with bad news.

The voice on the line sounds nervous, worried, and the words come in fits and starts. "I'm Nicolas's mom, I was trying to get hold of François, but his little sister explained that he'd gone to the market to work, so I told her I'd go there and see him, but then she said, 'Philippe is here, if you want to talk to him,' and I remembered that Nicolas had mentioned your name, in fact I think you've been to our house before and . . . And that stuck in my memory because he hardly ever invites anyone, so . . . So anyway . . . I know you all went to Saint-Martin together last night, for a birthday party, I think, and . . . and since Nicolas didn't come home last night, I wanted to find out if he slept at your house, or . . . I mean at François's house . . ."

Standing there naked in the living room, I don't see the blue of the sky on the other side of the window, all I see is the black of last night's sky, and I recite the events of the night almost mechanically: how everything was normal until Nicolas suddenly disappeared—there one minute, gone the next—and then vainly searching for him in the crowded club, and the discussion we had outside at three in the morning in the empty town, and the conclusion we came to—that he must have walked home on his own—and as I tell her all this, it rings so false in my ears and I realize it's all wrong because now I know that Nicolas didn't go home, and I understand how thoughtless we've been, how immature and irresponsible and cowardly.

And yet his mother doesn't get mad at me, or at least she doesn't yell down the phone line. She isn't mad at us because in reality she is already miles away, she's thinking about hanging up, calling the police, moving heaven and earth to find her son. Or she's already deep in some chasm, the earth giving way beneath her feet and swallowing her into its darkness. I mutter the meager words "Is there anything I can do to help?" When the truth is I know it's already too late, six hours too late, and we should have *done something* six hours ago, I should have *done something* when my instinct told me to, but I was too afraid of making a fool of myself, of causing a fuss, of worrying over nothing, and in the end we lost six hours that could have been precious.

She says: "Thanks, but it's okay, I'll deal with it."

And just after that, I hear the line go dead. I put the receiver back in its cradle. I'm lost in a haze for a moment and when I come out of it I see Virginie standing in the doorway. "You should probably put some clothes on," she says.

I run to the bedroom and get dressed. I need to go to the market and tell François. Not that he'll be able to do anything, of course, he'll be as helpless as I am, but I can't stay alone with this information, Nicolas's disappearance, it's impossible: if I stay alone with that, I'll go crazy. I don't plan to blame François or tell him "I told you so," not at all, because what would be the point? And the conclusion we came to last night made sense, it really did, perfect sense, and we're all in the same boat now anyway.

As I walk up Rue de la Cailletière toward Cours des Écoles, I notice that inside my mind concern is turning to panic, anxiety to alarm, and the fear spreading through my body is already becoming a terror that's beyond my powers to control. Trying to reason with myself, I think: He probably just ran away, he'll be back soon. Adolescents sometimes suffer with this languorous ennui that drives them away. (I wrote this—admittedly somewhat sententious—line, word for word, in a poem the previous summer, which undoubtedly proves that I believe it.) And if anyone was prey to languorous ennui, it was Nicolas.

And then I think about the hollyhocks, which were here yesterday and are still here today, and the permanence of things reassures me a little. But only a little.

When I get to the market, I stand outside the butcher van, behind three other customers waiting in line. For a moment or two I watch François, who's busy serving someone. When he notices me, he gives a little wave, smiles, and goes back to what he's doing. He's still safe in his ignorance, in his innocence. A wonderful state, I think, innocence. But you never realize how wonderful it is until you lose it.

Once the rush is over, I signal to him to come out and join me. As he's walking over, I see him wipe the blood from his hands on his apron. He looks at me, laughs, and says: "You're up earlier than I expected!"

I don't return his smile. I tell him about the phone call from Nicolas's mom.

He stares at me and says: "Fuck, are you kidding?"

At precisely two o'clock that afternoon, François, Christophe, Alice, Marc, and I are sitting on a row of chairs in a corridor of the Saint-Martin gendarmerie. We all received a phone call and were told to report here. We obeyed and now we're waiting nervously.

We've spent the whole morning hoping that Nicolas would reappear, but for the moment there's still no sign of him.

We can hardly look at each other. Not because we're embarrassed or ashamed, but simply because we're upset and we don't know how to handle this sort of emotion. And also because we're not used to being summoned to police stations, to all this gravity and solemnity. And probably because we can sense that something has been set in motion, something that is already beyond us. We can guess that there are people out searching. (Back then, there were no CCTV cameras, no cell phones, no secrets to be found inside computers, no credit cards that might betray the user's location. The police had to do the best they could with the limited resources to hand, and in truth their investigations were little more than bottles thrown out to sea.) We understand that the first interrogations have taken place, that various theories have been sketched out, and that we are part of this whole process. So we just glance around us, at the wanted posters, at the chairs lined up on the opposite wall, at the linoleum floor.

We don't speak either. We could be sharing our feelings, comparing memories, even interrupting each other because our heads are in turmoil and we're desperate not to forget anything or hide anything. But no, there's just this silence, as if our language has been stolen.

After we've been waiting there for quite a while, Alice leans her head against François's shoulder. This gesture doesn't mean anything, except perhaps—although this is huge in itself—a need for consolation. François doesn't move. He doesn't take advantage of the situation by putting his arm around Alice. He just lets her do it. The perfect gentleman. As for Marc, he briefly puts his hand on my thigh, and I turn and smile weakly at him. This is the only language remaining to us.

A few minutes later, we're sitting in a line again, but this time inside the captain's office. He looks about sixty, his gray hair cut short, and he's in uniform. And I'm sure that, to him, we look like a bunch of young idiots sitting there in front of him. Or, even worse, a bunch of pathetic, shamefaced young idiots. It seems to me that he is the archetype of serious adult authority, while we embody the fecklessness of youth.

Without any preamble, he summarizes the situation: "As you know, we have a missing person." I remember that expression, "we have a missing person," the way it sounded almost military in his mouth, as if a soldier had gone AWOL. Even so, it doesn't suggest death or violence, more the idea that the person has simply disappeared, evaporated, vanished into thin air.

He goes on, reading from a sheet on the desk in front of him: "Nicolas Tardieu, five feet nine, one hundred twenty-five pounds, blond hair, green eyes." For the captain, this must be a routine recap, an objective summary; for us, though, it's bewildering. First, because we know Nicolas, so we don't need to be told what he looks like. And second, because, hearing his vital statistics recited in this way, we understand that people—particularly *in circumstances like these*—can be described using physical characteristics.

It must have been his mother who provided these details. They asked her questions, presumably, the usual list of questions, and she gave them the answers they required. Because she knows the answers to those particular questions. She probably also gave them a photograph of her son, perhaps several. The investigators undoubtedly asked her to provide these. Did she have any recent pictures of her son? It's often the case that parents take lots of photographs of their children when they are babies or toddlers, but as they get older, this happens more rarely, not least because the kids themselves don't want to pose for photographs, or certainly not for their mother. Did she manage to steal a few moments to capture Nicolas's image without him realizing? If so, it would have been these stolen photographs that she gave to the police. Unless she managed to find a strip of Photomaton pictures, the kind that you have taken in a booth for your passport, for official forms, for high school.

The captain continues: "In order to complete the report, I will need you to provide me with information concerning the clothes he was wearing. His mother was unable to be very precise."

Then, to prevent us from forming the (false) impression that he is in any way blaming her for this inability, he adds: "Of course, she had no particular reason to pay close attention to her son's attire yesterday." Before concluding with the commonsense, horrifying words "She wasn't expecting not to see him again."

Alice is the one who answers, without hesitation: "He was wearing jeans, ripped at the knees, white Converse sneakers, and a plain purple T-shirt."

It's hard to tell if the captain doesn't entirely believe her or if he simply admires the precision of her memory. "You seem very sure of that, miss."

"I am sure," she replies confidently.

He probably thinks that girls care more about these things than boys, whereas the truth is that it's people in love who are more observant in this way, whose memories are more precise.

Now the policeman cuts to the chase. "Do you know what time it was when you last saw him?"

After conferring on this, we say: "Quarter past one in the morning."

He notes this down on his sheet of paper, then does a quick mental calculation. "So he's been missing for thirteen hours now."

A chill runs down our spines. We've seen enough movies and soap operas to know that the first hours are the crucial ones. Unconsciously this information must have imprinted itself on our brains. Until now, it never seemed like something that concerned us. Until now, we always believed that movies were just movies.

The officer continues to question us. "Would you say that he'd had a lot to drink? Just to be clear, I am not here to judge you or lecture you. If he'd had too much to drink, we are not going to blame anyone for that. Our objective is to find him, and to do that I need to know what kind of state he was in the last time you saw him."

"He'd had a couple of beers," I mumble. "No more than that. He wasn't a big drinker, Nicolas, and he could handle alcohol, so he wasn't drunk."

The others offer their loud agreement, but the policeman dampens our optimism. "You can't be certain of that, though, can you? Nobody was with him all night long?"

We admit that this is true. Then François adds: "You know what it's like—you don't stick together in a group all the time. Everyone does what he wants . . ."

(And already we are starting to feel guilty for this inattentiveness.)

Looking serious, the captain asks: "Did he seem okay to you? He wasn't feeling faint, for example?"

"You think he might have fallen, is that it?" François says, as if suddenly understanding. "You think he might have fallen from the battlements?"

The captain stares at us, appearing to weigh up whether or not he can trust us. Or maybe he's working out whether we're mature enough to hear what he has to say, or close enough to the missing person to merit being confided in. In the end, he says decisively: "You need to understand that it's my job to consider every possible hypothesis. Which obviously includes the possibility of an accident."

"But if he'd fallen, you would have found him," I object. "You'd have found his body."

He replies calmly: "That's the most plausible scenario, yes, but it takes time to search the coastline—"

I cut in: "You're searching the coastline?"

As calm as ever, he says: "Yes, some of my men have started going out in boats to watch for anomalies. So far, they haven't found anything."

"So he didn't fall," I conclude.

But he shakes his head. "We can't be sure of that, with the tides and currents in certain areas. We'll need to cover a bigger radius before we can be certain."

The phrase that sticks in my mind is *with the tides and currents in certain areas*. It's so vague that I find it unbearable, and I can't let it drop without saying something in return. And happily, I recall what Nicolas said to me at the Bastille Day dance, when he and I pissed from the battlements and I saw him sway and thought he was going to fall. I remember how he laughed and said: "I wouldn't have fallen, you know."

And this is what I shout at the policeman: "He wouldn't have fallen, you know. He's not like that. He's not the falling kind."

Even before the words are out of my mouth, I realize how absurd they sound, how baseless. The captain doesn't say anything, but the look he gives me makes clear what he thinks of my opinion.

I feel bad. But soon I feel even worse, as I remember what else Nicolas said to me that night: "That'd be a beautiful way to die." I force myself to believe that he was joking around, being a smart-ass. And I keep those ominous words to myself, because the last thing I want to do is confirm the captain's intuitions.

Even so, in my head I see the distorted, hypnotic image of Nicolas standing on a parapet, holding a plastic cup, mockingly observing the crowd on the dance floor—Alice walking away, Marc pulling me toward the restroom—unaware that he is too close to the edge, knocked off-balance by a sudden gust of wind . . . I decide to focus on the captain's questions.

"Did anything else happen last night that struck you as out of the ordinary?"

We look at each other but can't think of anything. The

fact that Alice was trying (and failing) to get in Nicolas's pants doesn't seem like the kind of information the policeman is seeking. It happens all the time, these misunderstandings between girls and boys—one not liking the other enough, or the two of them not liking each other at the same time, or not being compatible in some way—and it's never a big problem. Even though Nicolas did strike me as a complex, sensitive guy, I can't imagine him being deeply shaken by this episode. Not enough to do anything stupid, anyway. All the same, I notice that Alice is looking sheepish, as though wishing she hadn't pressured him like that.

"What about in the days leading up to last night?" the captain asks.

We just continue to stare at the floor, our only response a frown or a shrug.

Abruptly he loses his temper. "Come on, this is important! We're urgently investigating a missing minor, so if you know anything, you need to tell me—and tell me now. And if nothing comes to mind, then *think*! Make an effort! We don't have any time to lose here."

We're all shocked by this little speech. Still, we suspect he's probably right, and that he knows what he's doing. And the truth is, we haven't really thought about it. Why would we? This is what it means to be eighteen, after all: to live in the moment, without having to drag the past around with you, even the very recent past, and to be carefree, not weighed down by the seriousness of things, not bothering to pay attention to details because it seems to us that the details don't really matter, and on top of that we don't really know yet what does matter.

The others look around the room or through the window, trying to catch a glimpse of the outside world, perhaps hoping that it will come to their rescue. I look down, and notice that the laces of one of my sneakers have come undone. In my mind, those untied laces are the perfect illustration of our pathetic helplessness.

And as I sink deeper into this well of misery, my memory snags on one of the terms used by the captain when he was shouting at us: *minor*.

"Nicolas is a minor?" I say.

The policeman doesn't hide his frustration. "Is that the only thing you remember from what I said to you?! And how come you didn't know that, anyway? I thought this guy was your 'friend'?" Breathing hard, he checks the sheet on his desk. "Nicolas Tardieu, born August thirty-first, 1967. So yes, he'll turn eighteen in just over a month."

I realize then that we never asked him when his birthday was. Not when we were talking about driver's licenses or when we were planning Christophe's birthday. Nobody thought about it. The idea never crossed our mind. The cop is right: we didn't really know Nicolas. Or not well enough, anyway.

François, as if reading my mind, and visibly irritated by the captain's words, says defiantly: "He is our friend. You don't have to memorize someone's birth certificate to be friends with them."

The captain takes a deep breath, and when he speaks again he sounds as calm and precise as before. "Okay, let's take this step-by-step. For example, did he ever talk to you about his high school?"

"He talked to me about it sometimes, yeah," volunteers François.

The policeman signals for him to keep talking.

François looks puzzled. "What do you want me to say?"

"Well, did he have problems there?"

François still doesn't seem to understand, so I come to his aid. "I think he wants to know if Nicolas got in trouble at school. If he stole stuff or took drugs or whatever. Right?"

François instantly shoots this down. "No, that wasn't his kind of thing at all. He'd have told me if he was doing stuff like that."

"Are you sure about that?" the policeman asks skeptically. "Would you say that Nicolas was the type of kid who shared his secrets?"

François lowers his eyes.

And then, suddenly, I remember something. Like a light bulb going on inside my head. I'm so excited that I startle the others by yelling: "There was a guy last night, at Le Bastion! A guy from his high school, he said, this jerk who— Sorry, sir, I only say that because that's the word Nicolas used, I wouldn't say it otherwise . . . Anyway, Nicolas didn't want this guy to see him there." .

The captain looks hopeful. "Do you know what he looked like, this . . . 'guy'?"

"No, sorry, I didn't see him," I say. "I could just tell that it had a big effect on Nicolas when he saw him. A really big effect."

"And yet you told me earlier that nothing out of the ordinary happened," the captain points out crossly.

"I'd forgotten that," I explain. "It just came back to me now. It struck me as weird when it happened and afterward it slipped my mind, but now that you're asking us about his high school . . ."

I realize that the captain is, in his own way, guiding us toward something. Under his supervision, we are putting together the pieces of a puzzle. And I'm afraid of what the picture will look like once we've completed it.

"All right, we'll look into it," he says. "You never know . . ." Then he tells us: "His mother says he's never run away before. Did he ever talk to any of you about running away? Even if he sounded like he was joking around?"

We're surprised by this question, although I feel certain that all of us have privately considered the possibility. The truth is we don't want anyone to put our secret fears into clear, precise words. All five of us shake our heads.

But then Christophe says: "Actually, he did say something

weird to me once . . . But he was probably just messing around, you know . . ."

François and I immediately understand what Christophe is alluding to.

The policeman stares at him. "Tell me anyway."

"I was saying that being a fisherman is a boring job, and that sometimes I think about leaving, but I couldn't, and he said 'You can always leave' or something like that. But, like I said, it wasn't anything big, and it doesn't really have anything to do with what you asked us . . ."

The policeman carefully writes this down on the page in front of him. And we just sit there, listening to the squeak of his marker on the paper.

I dare to ask: "Have you found something that makes you suspect he's run away? I'm guessing you went to his house and searched his room . . . So did you see anything that suggests he was planning to leave? Did he take any of his stuff, for example? I mean, if you're going away for a while, you'd pack a bag or something, right?"

The others stare at me with a mixture of astonishment and admiration as they become aware—at the same time as me, I admit—that I'm capable of thinking like a detective. The captain smiles at me. "You're right, young man, we did do all of that. But we didn't find anything."

In reality, I'm so desperate for nothing bad to have happened to Nicolas that I'm almost automatically trying to shoot down any theory I don't like, trying to convince myself that everything is normal.

(Except, of course, that there is absolutely nothing normal about Nicolas's prolonged absence.)

The captain, though, pours cold water on my hopeful hypothesis. "You know, sometimes people run away because they're scared, because they feel threatened, because they feel like they have no other option, and when that happens they don't take anything with them because they don't have the time, or the opportunity. Did Nicolas Tardieu seem scared to you?"

Now that we have something worse to consider—the idea that our friend might have fled in a panic because he was being bullied or blackmailed, the idea that he might have done something bad that forced him to take off—the theory that he simply ran away strikes me as much more palatable. Even an accident wouldn't be so bad: lots of people have an accident and still survive. I realize that it has taken only a few minutes for what I refused to imagine to be relegated to the rank of a lesser evil.

And so, shocked into docility, we start to rack our brains. We try to recall whether Nicolas ever said anything about being scared, whether he mentioned an enemy, all the while trying not to think too deeply about what any of this might mean.

It doesn't take me long to remember what he told me about his father: the violence, the fact that they had to leave town. And I see again the crossed-out drawing that I found in his bedroom yesterday, when I entered that empty, silent house. I don't dare mention this, because I don't know

Nicolas's father, and all fathers—even the bastards—seem to demand a certain respect. But then I catch the captain eyeing me impatiently, and I murmur: "I think he had a difficult relationship with his father . . ."

"What are you talking about?" François asks angrily.

I shrug. "That's what he told me . . ."

François stares at me as if seeing me for the first time in his life, but I'm not sure what bothers him most: the idea that I'm a snitch or that Nicolas confided in me.

The captain makes calming motions with his hands. "We already know about that. His mother told us all about it."

"So we're back to square one, then," says François.

A beam of sunlight pours through the window, casting a shard of brightness on the brown linoleum that blinds us for a fraction of a second. We almost forgot about the outside world, about life going on.

When we focus on the captain again, we notice, for the first time, that he looks embarrassed, and this change in his expression is enough to alarm me. I realize that nothing—in this office, in these circumstances—can possibly be neutral or benign, and my senses grow more alert.

He clears his throat. "There's a question I have to ask you . . . I'm sure you understand that, in an investigation like this, we can't rule out any possibility . . . All the same, I want you to know that I am not saying that this is likely . . . But . . . Did Nicolas ever talk to you about . . . *the idea of suicide?* . . . Once again, I am not saying this is likely . . . In fact, I'm hoping you can help us to eliminate this theory, in a way . . ."

(There is something delicate about the way he frames this: the suggestion that suicide is merely an idea, a concept, almost an abstraction.)

There's no point lying to ourselves: of course this possibility has crossed our minds—we're made in such a way that we can't completely ignore our darkest fears—but we tried to immediately get rid of the thought, at least out of superstition, so it wouldn't come true. We felt bad, not for having entertained the idea but for having done so in secret, and now it has come back to haunt us, articulated by a third party, by an adult in uniform.

"No signs of depression?" the captain asks. "No traumatic experiences that you know of? Morbid tendencies? Visible scars? No particular fascination with famous suicides?"

We are frightened by this list, which sounds as though it has been taken from some sort of textbook, written by specialists—and it probably has. We say no to all of it. Because it's the truth (as far as we know), or because saying no is a way of putting an end to this horrible speculation?

(Even so, I try to picture Nicolas's body in my mind, searching it for scars, bruises, wounds. And I admit that the body is a metaphor.)

I turn to Alice and see tears in the corners of her eyes. She wipes them away with the back of her hand.

At this very moment, the telephone rings, providing us with a welcome diversion. The captain answers it. We don't know who he's talking to. The only phrases that stick in our minds are "searching," "called all the hospitals," "appeal for witnesses," "missing person alert."

This is it, I think. Things are getting serious now. Something is going on, something we don't understand, and we will play only a minor, secondary role from now on. All we can do is leave it to the experts and wait for an outcome. The future will depend on their investigations, their interrogations, the vast machine of their cross-checking procedures. This thought makes me swallow, makes me feel dizzy and nauseated, makes the blood beat hard in my temples. I look around this large, soulless office with its metal filing cabinets, its Venetian blinds, its gray walls, its official photograph of the president of the French Republic, and I see how tiny and insignificant we are in all of this.

The captain hangs up, and seeing the expressions on our faces—like a group of guilty schoolkids—he guesses that his words have scared us. So he does his best to reassure us: "Don't worry, it's just normal procedure. We have rules for this sort of situation. And that's a good thing, having rules."

He's talking to us as if we're children. No doubt because we look exactly like children to him.

"We're still hoping for a rapid and happy resolution to the case. We see it all the time: people disappear, then they reappear soon afterward."

"Really?" Alice asks incredulously.

"Oh yes, happens all the time," he says. "People who want to seem interesting, to see how popular they are. Or people who fall into a black hole. Or just slightly sad, lost people."

I don't believe that Nicolas wanted to seem interesting and I know that he couldn't have cared less how popular he was. I don't know what a black hole is; I imagine it as a momentary liberation from reality, a separation from the world, but I have no idea how it comes about. I wouldn't rule out the sadness thing though. I feel almost certain that Nicolas carries his sadness around with him. Even Virginie, at only thirteen, noticed that, didn't she, when she said that he was "broken inside"?

"So are we done here?" the captain asks, peering at us one by one. "Nothing to add? Is there anything else you might have forgotten, anything that might help us find your friend? No? Okay, well, if anything comes back to you, this is our phone number. Don't hesitate to call us, all right?"

He stands up, and after a brief delay, so do we. Chair legs squeak on linoleum. He accompanies us to the door. "Ah, actually I do have one last question. Did Nicolas ever mention the existence of a place that he liked to go when he wanted to be alone?"

We all look at each other but, again, we have no answer to give him. We leave the gendarmerie, feeling useless.

We have been infected by the town's agitation, its noises and odors, and it takes us a while to get used to the more familiar sights of people lounging outside restaurants after finishing their moules-frites, people strolling along sidewalks glancing in the windows of clothing boutiques or gift shops, people eating ice cream or waffles as they wander along the quays, people going off to the beach, or new vacationers arriving because today is Saturday. We're surprised that all of this is going on as normal. Because, for us, there is nothing normal about what's happening. So we just stand there, arms hanging by our sides, not knowing what to do with our bodies.

It's François who drags us out of our torpor. "We're not far from La Martinière, you know. Why don't we go get an ice cream?"

A few minutes later, we're sitting around a circular table containing two cafés liégeois, one peach melba, one dame blanche, and one poire belle Hélène, along with some langue de chat cookies, and a multicolored paper umbrella planted in the top scoop of ice cream on each dessert. (La Martinière had a room where you could sit, back then, and watch the day go by. Nowadays, it's just a streetside countertop, looking out at the port.)

I remember that, for me, as a child, this place used to seem like an Aladdin's cave. Christian would bring me here and let me choose whatever I wanted. I'd take forever to pick, hesitating between several different flavors, making the waitress stand around when she should have been serving all the other tables and all the other children, before I finally decided and then had to go through the torture of waiting for the object of my desire to be brought to me. I would devour my ice cream as soon as they set it in front of me. At first, I'd attack it so fast that it gave me brain freeze—like a thread of pure cold pain running from deep inside my skull to the edge of my eye socket—but thankfully that would disappear as quickly as it had appeared. No matter how many times Christian reminded me to eat slowly, I never listened to him. Now this memory is almost enough to make me throw up. La Martinière no longer belongs to the geography of my pampered childhood, but to that of our ruined adolescence.

Presumably, François suggested coming here because he thought it would "take our minds off" the situation. Sadly, it fails completely, because we can think of nothing else. Nothing but Nicolas. The ice cream does nothing to lighten our shock or anguish.

And, inevitably, we soon return to our morbid game of hypothesizing. Worse than that, freed from the protective, paralyzing presence of the captain, we scratch at the scab of our fears.

What we dread most is the idea of a stupid accident. Alice is the first to mention the possibility that he simply fell from the battlements. "Let's be honest, it could have happened, especially at one in the morning, after a few drinks . . . Or someone could have bumped into him and knocked him over the edge without even realizing, because there were so many completely wrecked guys in that club, or they could have knocked him over and not told anyone when they realized how much trouble they'd be in."

"But someone would have seen that, right?" I protest.

"It could have happened farther off," Alice says, "out toward the lighthouse. There wouldn't have been so many people around at that time of night."

(Clearly, she's been giving this some thought, and that in itself is evidence of the desire she felt for him, not to mention the disappointment that followed. Some trace of these emotions subsists.)

We all think: Yeah, okay, that's possible.

Marc says: "It wouldn't necessarily kill you—it's not that high!"

But Christophe makes a face at this. "Honestly? If you fell headfirst onto the rocks . . ."

We are horrified by this image.

Marc insists: "But they'd have found his body, if that was true. I don't believe all that crap about currents."

"You're wrong," says Christophe. "When the tide goes out, the currents are really strong. And they would take you south."

At that remark, our last hopes suddenly give way.

"In that case," I say, "you have to consider the possibility that someone deliberately pushed him."

"What the fuck!" exclaims François.

"Think about it," I say. "He saw this guy who he didn't want to be seen by. What if they bumped into each other and got into a fight?"

"You can get into a fight without throwing the other person into the sea!" François protests.

I decide to refresh his memory. "What about that guy you had an argument with last year at the campsite? I don't even remember what you were arguing about, but you were fucking furious with him. You wanted to shove his head down the toilet!"

He shrugs. "I'd never have done it, though."

There are punch-ups every summer, fights between the

tourists and the locals, and the protagonists are almost always teenagers. The cocktail of darkness, alcohol, and sweltering humidity invariably sets them off.

"Well, I think he's run away," decides Alice. "That's the most likely scenario, right?"

We all loudly agree.

"He's kind of weird, Nico, don't you think?"

Again, everyone agrees (and I deduce from this that Alice has a thing for weird guys). But I can't help questioning the new consensus. "Wouldn't we have guessed that something was up? If he was planning to run away, I mean?"

"He's an enigma," says Alice. "He doesn't open much, does he? When you're secretive like that, you could hide anything from your friends."

"Or maybe we just weren't paying attention," I suggest.

It's true that we don't pay enough attention to other people—to their private, hidden suffering, to the distress signals they sometimes send us—because we're so focused on ourselves, so preoccupied with our own pleasure, our own worries. We prefer to turn a blind eye, since it's so much easier, or we're wary of "getting worked up over nothing" because we're young and it's summer, and you shouldn't take things too seriously in the summer. But when it comes down to it, this nonchalance can easily tip over into neglect.

Later, alone, I will be tortured by all these cruel what-ifs.

What if, on that fateful Saturday, we'd decided to spend

the night at Christophe's house instead, to take advantage of the fact that his parents had gone to visit a sick aunt on the mainland? What if we'd just lazed around on the living room couch watching *Indiana Jones*? We'd spotted it on VHS a few days before and thought about buying it. And Christophe was so proud of the family's new VCR . . .

What if, that terrible night, I hadn't snuck off to kiss Marc in a toilet stall, caught up in the illusory joys of the moment, but had instead kept my eye on Nicolas?

What if I'd paid more attention to his silences, his guarded anxieties? What if I'd understood that nonchalance is sometimes just a mask we wear to conceal our inner turmoil?

Yes, maybe he'd left us clues, however tenuous, and we simply hadn't picked up on them. *I* hadn't picked up on them.

"Or maybe the cop was right," Christophe says, "and it was a last-minute decision. Maybe something happened and he just took off."

François looks doubtful. "But what could have happened to make him run off like that?"

"How should I know?" replies Christophe. "Maybe he made a mistake and it came back to haunt him . . ."

I frown skeptically. "In a nightclub? At one in the morning?"

"Oh, whatever!" grunts Christophe, exasperated by all our doubts.

Then Marc gets involved, saying mysteriously: "Or maybe it has something to do with his father . . ."

The others shout him down, with François sneering that he's been reading too many *Famous Five* books.

I am the only one to defend the idea. "Actually, Nicolas told me that his dad had threatened to show up here, and he said he was a difficult person. He didn't go into details, but he definitely talked about violence."

The others draw closer, and Alice says in a whisper: "You mean he'd have come to the island? To do what?"

"Maybe Nicolas saw him just before we went out?" suggests Marc. "He seemed like he was miles away, remember?"

"But then what?" Alice prompts.

"Well," says Marc, appearing to enjoy his own fiction, "if his dad was threatening to take him home—to get back at his mom, or maybe for some other reason—then Nicolas might have run away . . ."

"Oh, what a load of crap!" says François. "This is real life, not a movie."

"Maybe it is crap," I say, shrugging. "Maybe not. The problem is that anything's plausible."

The one theory that nobody dares talk about is suicide. I mean, who kills himself at seventeen?

Night has fallen, François and I have gone back to the house, and Nicolas has now been missing for twenty-one hours.

We stay in the kitchen after dinner, sitting either side of the table. François took a can of Coke out of the fridge but he hasn't touched it. I roll a ball of breadcrumbs between the tip of my index finger and the waxed tablecloth until the ball is darkened by grime. We don't speak. We barely even look at each other.

We know that there's a missing person alert out for Nicolas, but that they haven't found anything yet. We know that the local hospitals have all been called, in vain, and that the police might use a dog to help them search.

Our parents have gone to sit in the living room and we can hear their whispered conversation. They're talking about the disappearance, of course. Earlier, during dinner, they'd expressed to us their dismay and their sympathy, saying things like "Oh, it's so horrible." They'd tried to sound optimistic, to avoid speculation. Now, though, the floodgates have been opened.

Christian goes first: "You have to wonder if the kid was mixed up in something shady."

"What sort of thing?" my father asks.

"Drugs," Christian replies bluntly. "Maybe he was taking them secretly. Maybe he was dealing. Maybe he was hanging around with the wrong sort of people. We all know that there are gangsters behind that shit."

"I don't know, people would have noticed if a teenage kid was dealing drugs, wouldn't they?" my father says. "Surely his mother would have realized something was going on . . ."

"You're kidding, right?" Christian ripostes. "Our kids are the best in the world when it comes to doing stuff in secret and pulling the wool over our eyes."

Anne-Marie pipes up: "Look at François, he started smoking. He didn't tell us, obviously, I just found out by chance one day when I was driving through town and I saw him standing by the carousel, smoking a cigarette. He didn't see me."

François smiles—a thin, weary, half-hearted smile—and whispers: "Of course I saw her—I recognized the car. How dumb does she think I am?"

I think about what I hid for a long time, what I ended up admitting only when I couldn't lie anymore, and I know that anyone is capable of deceiving the people around them.

This is so true that I can't say for sure whether Nicolas was taking drugs or not. I have the feeling he wasn't, but there's no way to know and that really bothers me. I feel just like our parents, confessing their ignorance of their children's lives. I too am lost—so lost that it makes my head spin.

Christian doesn't stop there; he's already dreaming up another scenario. "Or maybe he was abducted by some pervert—there are lunatics everywhere, especially in summer. All these sleazy-looking guys prowling around, and you never know who they are."

"You think?" my father says skeptically.

"Of course!" Christian hisses. "You've seen that stuff on TV, haven't you? The pedophiles and rapists . . . Why should we be spared? Why wouldn't it happen here too?"

Only parents, only adults, could imagine such horrors, we think. It has never crossed our minds. The truth is we don't know much about the darkness of the human soul. We hardly ever listen to the news. And we trust people, we give them the benefit of the doubt, we don't see lunatics everywhere. It's not that we're naïve, just that it's simpler and more relaxing to assume that other people aren't monsters. We will lose our illusions later in life.

Then Christian's imagination goes into overdrive and he says anxiously: "Or what if he had his head turned by those weirdos . . . what do you call them again? Gurus, that's it. Apparently there are more and more sects around these days."

"Christian, you're just babbling now," my father says, ever the rationalist.

But Christian doesn't back down. "You're telling me you've never heard of those crazy guys who lure gullible kids into their clutches by promising them a return to nature or whatever, then take them into the woods and they're never seen again?"

"But . . ." My father sounds like he's suddenly doubting himself. "I don't know, there would have been warning signs, wouldn't there?"

"How well do we even know this kid, though? He and his mother only came to the island last winter. They're from Tours or Poitiers and I've heard that they had problems there. Like, not your normal problems . . ."

This makes me think. I think about how nice we are to people's faces and how mean we can be about them the moment their back's turned. I think about other people's bad reputations and how they make us believe we're the good guys. A tragedy like this can bring out the worst in people, and for the first time in my life I find myself disliking Christian.

My mother is the one who defends the Tardieu family. "I can't help thinking about his poor mother, all alone at home tonight, desperately hoping for a sign of life. She's probably in her son's bedroom, waiting for him to come home, wondering what could have happened to him . . . It must be driving her crazy. Or maybe she's calling people, like family and friends, to find out if they've heard anything. I can't imagine she'll get much sleep tonight. Or any night for a while to come."

Silence falls in the living room. I picture them all looking chastened.

And here we can sense the age-old fear of all parents: the terror of losing a child.

Suddenly, out of nowhere, Virginie appears in the kitchen. She's heard about Nicolas. She stands in front of us and says: "I've been thinking about it, and what if he's lost his memory? Don't laugh! These things happen, you know. I saw a film on France One, an American film about a guy who banged his head and got amnesia. All of a sudden he didn't know his own name or where he lived. So obviously he couldn't go home or tell anyone."

"Sure, why not," I say gently. "Except that life isn't an American film."

She shrugs irritably.

Without even glancing at his sister, François says: "I'm beat. Let's go to bed."

He stands up and walks away and I follow him. A few seconds later we're lying on our beds in the dark. We don't talk. I can hear his breathing, so I know he hasn't fallen asleep, and he must know that I haven't either.

I try to understand why this disappearance has hit me so hard. Obviously, it's a worrying situation, but I only met Nicolas ten days ago—I ought to be capable of putting it into some kind of perspective. I ought to be concerned, but not overwhelmed like this. Unfortunately, that's not how it works.

Yet again, it's as if François can read my mind. "It's true that we didn't know him that well," he says, "but we were there when he vanished. We were right there, for fuck's sake!"

On Sunday a search party is hurriedly organized by the police, backed up by the local fire department—a sign that this disappearance is being taken seriously and that hopes are not high.

There are also about forty volunteers to help conduct the search. Not as many as you might expect, but Nicolas's mother is a recent arrival and she doesn't know many people. And it's summer. In summer, people have other things to do.

The police corral us into groups and send us off in various directions. They've outlined a priority zone, based on information that has not been communicated to us, and we're told to methodically search our assigned area. In theory, we are looking for clues—"pieces of fabric, personal belongings, footprints"—but we all understand that the real aim is, at best, to find Nicolas lying unconscious somewhere, at worst to find his corpse.

So we walk along shaded tracks, through undergrowth carpeted with pine needles, across weed-strewn fields, eyes fixed to the arid, sandy ground. We search abandoned buildings, investigate ditches, jump over streams, push aside tall grass, all the while looking around differently at these

173

familiar landscapes, aware that they could, for the first time, break our hearts.

I walk unsteadily, praying that I will not hear a voice in the distance yelling that they've "found something." Praying that I won't discover Nicolas's body myself. My heart skips a beat when I spot a shape a few feet away, but it turns out to be a small hill. Occasionally I glance sideways at François, who looks simultaneously diligent and resigned.

The whole scene strikes me as surreal, stupefying. I can't believe we're actually living through this. When I force myself to think about it more objectively, to contemplate this moment as if I weren't part of it, the madness of the situation seems even more obvious. We shouldn't be here. We're not prepared for this sort of thing. We're not cut out for it. We're in over our heads. We're scared. And yet here we are, moving forward, concentrated, meticulous, obeying orders that are both precise and insane. The only thing I know for sure is that we will remember this, because it is, literally, unforgettable. And I don't think we're going to come out of it unscathed. Our lives have been carefree and pure, but that is changing now. We are losing our innocence. Yes, I think, this is it: the end of innocence.

At three in the afternoon, the search is officially ended. "We're not going to find anything," says a man in uniform. I don't know whether to be depressed or relieved by this. All I know is that Nicolas's absence has become even more undeniable. Before, it was a vanishing act. Now it's an erasure.

Before, he was missing; now we're missing him. The

emotion surges up and bites us. Not to see him again—this mysterious blond boy, this endearing friend—seems suddenly, and for the first time, unbearable.

Back in Place des Tilleuls, we see three men coming out of L'Escale. Bursting out of it, I should say, very excited and visibly the worse for wear. They punch the air and yell that Bernard Hinault has just won his fifth Tour de France.

François mutters: "Who gives a fuck?"

It's incredible: Nicolas is walking toward me, smiling and waving his hand. Is he beckoning me over? Or maybe he's making fun of me, speaking words that I don't hear.

The image repeats: he comes forward, makes a gesture with his hand, pats down his hair, and I can't reach him. And it starts over again at the beginning, as if a video has been rewound and replayed, a video without sound. The image haunts me, obsesses me, it repeats endlessly in a loop.

And then I wake up.

Only in my dream does Nicolas put one foot in front of the other, smiling ineffably.

I'm alone in the silent bedroom. When I get out of bed, I feel numb. A shower will do me a world of good, I think. I stand under the jet of hot water for a long time, thinking of nothing, concentrating on my glistening, tanned skin.

I drink a cup of coffee, standing in the kitchen. Through the window I see my parents, sitting at the garden table: my father is reading his newspaper, my mother doing a crossword. I should be reassured to discover that life goes on, that it can go on, but instead I am filled with dismay. The truth is that I resent them for their indifference, although how are they supposed to behave? I tell myself to stop being so stupid: there's no point blaming them. Suddenly, they both look up at the same time. I follow their gaze, and to my surprise I see Marc standing in front of the garden gate. I guess that he's asking them if I'm home, so I go out to meet him.

I kiss my parents on the cheeks before telling Marc: "Let's go inside." My mother glances in our direction, clearly wondering about this athletic boy and his relationship to her son. (With hindsight, I know that she wasn't wondering anything: she knew.)

As soon as we're in the living room, he tells me why he's here. "We're leaving the island this afternoon."

I stare at him in stupefaction. "I thought you weren't leaving till next Saturday."

"Alice doesn't want to stay here anymore," he explains. "She said she couldn't imagine going to the beach or the café as if nothing had happened. She begged our parents to take us somewhere else, and they agreed. So we're going to stay with some friends in Deauville."

(Of course they have "friends in Deauville." Of course they can change their vacation plans at the drop of a hat.)

"It's crazy," he says. "I think she's lost all hope that Nicolas will ever come back. In fact, I know she has. We were having breakfast together this morning and she said: 'We'll never see him again.' I said that was stupid, she didn't know anything about it, he'd only been gone two days, but she wouldn't listen. She said something about intuition . . . Yeah, that's it, she said she had an intuition that he wouldn't come back. She even said something fucked up, I don't even know if I should tell you . . ." But he does. "She said: 'I wouldn't be surprised if François pushed him. Out of jealousy.' I told her she was talking crap. Then she suddenly apologized and said this whole thing was driving her crazy, not knowing what's really happened."

I am speechless. What Alice dared to say about François, even surreptitiously, even if you could put it down to her shock and confusion, makes me hate her. Marc senses this, and he puts his hand in front of my mouth to prevent me from saying anything I can't take back. I slowly turn my face to free myself from his grip. Then, looking at the floor, I just whisper: "It's wrong, just leaving like this, so soon. When someone goes missing, you should wait for them to come back. At least for a while." And then, in my head, I repeat Alice's premonition: We'll never see him again.

I decide to change the subject. "You could stay, though, right? You could join them later . . ."

He smiles weakly. "I'd love to, but . . ."

We step closer and he holds my face between his hands. We kiss. There's real tenderness in this kiss, no doubt about it, and nobody is more bewildered by this than me, because— after Thomas—I'd decided I wouldn't fall for the first boy I met, that I wouldn't mix up lust and love. But I can't deny it: what I feel is overwhelming.

And then I realize that this is a goodbye kiss. I realize that Marc and I will never see each other again, even if we yield to the idiotic impulse to promise each other that we will. I realize that something is ending. It wasn't a big deal—just a brief fling, a summer crush, silly and sublime—but the truth is that, even at eighteen, I find it hard to deal with endings.

I wish I could make him stay a little longer, my blond tennis player. I wish I could drag him upstairs to the bedroom and undress him, or even suck him off here, now, in the living room. I wish we could be overcome by sensuality, by animal passion, but I let the kiss end and I watch him leave.

That afternoon, sprawled out on the couch, I try to take my mind off things by chatting with Virginie. She must see right through my pathetic little stratagem because she doesn't mention the disappearance. Instead, she spends ages talking about the Italian pop star Eros Ramazzotti, swearing hand on heart that it is not a betrayal of her beloved Modern Talking, that she loves them too. The next thing I know, she's going on about some TV show. I tell her I've never seen it. "Well, don't bother," she advises me. "It's getting worse and worse." When she realizes that I'm not really listening, she moves closer to me and whispers: "It's normal that you're sad. But sadness doesn't help, does it?"

I stare at her, taken aback, and I don't know whether to smile or cry.

Then she adds calmly: "Besides, we guessed it would end this way . . ."

I'm so stunned by this that I can't speak at first, but just as I'm about to ask her what she means, François appears in the doorway and tells me, in a tone that brooks no argument, that we're going to Grenettes. So I have to regretfully leave Virginie and her crystal ball to follow her brother, because I can sense that he is also seeking a diversion, an escape, a way back to our old carefree lives.

It was at Grenettes, though, that we met up with Nicolas on that very first day, when I arrived on the island. It was here that I first got to know him. I don't bring up this memory to François. Maybe he's forgotten, I think. But when we sit on the beach, leaning against the split-rail fence, I can tell—from his clenched jaw—that it's all coming back to him. He doesn't say anything though.

We watch the people on the beach, the massed bodies, the rows of towels, the parasols stuck in the sand, the parents keeping a close eye on their toddlers, the girls nodding to the music from their Walkmans, the boys battling the big waves, the glimmering water, the boats anchored out at sea, and without warning François murmurs: "I regret what I said about him. Thin as a rake, silent and weird, all that stuff. I feel like a jerk."

"That's just misplaced guilt," I say.

He looks irritated at this and says: "Come on, let's get out of here."

As we head back to La Noue, the sun in our eyes, he grumbles: "Have you noticed how nobody talks about it anymore? Nobody gives a fuck, in fact."

(Back then, there were no twenty-four-hour news channels or social media echo chambers endlessly recycling everyday horrors, making money from emotion, fabricating fantasies, stoking psychosis.)

I have to admit that the incomprehensible disappearance

of a teenager seems to have caused nothing more than a brief gasp of shock, a fleeting ripple of sympathy, before being brushed away like sand from skin. It isn't even a topic of conversation anymore.

François suggests that we should go and see Nicolas's mother.

I can't hide my astonishment at this. "And say what to her?"

"I don't know," he says, looking defeated.

Even so, we walk toward Rue des Chênes. As we're approaching the house, François freezes. He stares at the façade, unmoving, then turns to me. "You're right, what are we going to say?"

We immediately retrace our steps. The street is deserted at this time of day. Our solitude feels vast.

The next day, unable to stand it anymore, I decide to call the captain at the gendarmerie. The receptionist asks me to wait, and I do, for a long time. He must be busy, or maybe he just can't be bothered talking to some anxious teenager? In the end, to my surprise—perhaps out of pity—he agrees to speak with me, after making it clear that he doesn't have much time and that he will not go into details of the case with anyone other than the boy's family, conditions that I accept without difficulty. I don't want him to hang up on me right away, so I start by questioning him about the information I gave him: the presence of that boy at Le Bastion, the one that Nicolas didn't want to see.

He responds unhesitatingly: "We talked to his mother about that and she made the connection: you were right, he's a boy from Nicolas's high school, Patrice Augier, and we discovered that they had a . . . conflictual relationship, let's say. In fact, this Patrice Augier spent the whole year bullying Nicolas. From what I understand, he would regularly make fun of his appearance, calling him 'effeminate' and so on. He would make fun of his love of art too, and one day he even grabbed his portfolio and threw his drawings all over the schoolyard, and since Nicolas didn't have many friends, nobody came to his rescue. I get the impression he was very isolated, and since he's not exactly the athletic type he never defended himself either, and you know, if you don't defend yourself, the bullies will just keep bullying you. And on top of that, it's a . . . difficult high school, shall we say. There's a lack of discipline there, and the bullies can get away with it. Like this Patrice Augier, who, unsurprisingly, failed his baccalaureate, and so, you see, he would be in Nicolas's class again this September . . ."

At the other end of the line, I am dumbstruck by this little speech. First, I visualize the scenes: I picture Nicolas being shoved in a corridor, provoked, intimidated. I see the drawings scattered all over the schoolyard. I hear the insults, the swearing, the crude remarks. I imagine how it must feel to go through this, day after day. But I don't have to imagine it, do I? Because I've lived through all of this. I know it by heart. I know how tempting it is to withdraw into yourself, how isolation can come to seem the only way to bear the constant abuse.

Also, I'm discovering a different Nicolas. Or rather I'm realizing that every aspect of his personality that I noticed before has an underside: that his shyness is a kind of fear, or the memory of fear; that his silence is a difficulty in speaking; that his gentleness is a fragility, his solitude a form of exclusion, his feminine beauty a burden; and that his drawings are a cry for help, a cry that we didn't hear.

Again I find myself thinking about the things people tell

us between their words that we don't understand, about what they show us of themselves that we don't see, because we're busy doing something else or simply distracted, because another person's life doesn't interest us that much, or because the swimmer, far out to sea, who appears to be waving to us is actually drowning. I think about our indifference, our offhandedness, toward others, and how, most of the time, this has no consequences, but sometimes it does. I think about the people we let leave without understanding that they are silently begging us to make them stay.

The captain, no doubt oblivious to all these thoughts, continues speaking: "We questioned this Patrice Augier. He was dumbstruck, literally, when he found out what had happened to Nicolas. He swore to us he hadn't even seen him there, and . . . well, he seemed sincere . . . No, that's not quite right: what I mean is, he's too stupid to lie convincingly . . . And his friends all say they were with him all night and that they didn't see Nicolas either. There were almost five hundred people in the club, so it's perfectly plausible."

I don't know what to think about this. I would like this Patrice guy to lose some sleep over what might happen to him, but I don't really want him to be found guilty of anything. I want an answer, but not that one. The simplest thing is to trust the police, I think.

"So what did happen that night?" I ask. "Nicolas left and fell off the battlements somewhere?"

The captain clears his throat. For a few seconds he's silent, then finally he says: "As you know, the search we conducted was fruitless. We've now expanded the area that we're searching. We've been through the woods, we've dragged the saltwater marshes, we've inspected churches, abandoned houses, old bunkers, and so on, but we haven't found anything."

I hear myself whisper: "So maybe he was abducted?"

There's silence on the other end of the line again. It goes on for longer this time. And then: "This is a peaceful place."

This argument strikes me as so weak that it instantly makes my hypothesis seem credible. It bothers me so much that I change the subject. "And his father? Have you questioned him? Have you been to his house?"

"I'm not supposed to provide you with that kind of information."

"Come on . . . please?"

"We checked him out. Nothing."

"What about your appeal for witnesses? Did anyone come forward?"

"Some people, yes, but it didn't provide any serious leads. People think they've seen something, but in reality what they saw was something else, or someone else, or they think something's a clue when it's really nothing of the kind. We were even approached by a fortune teller offering to find him using tarot cards."

I sigh.

Hearing this, the captain tries to reassure and console me. "Of course, there may have been clues we've missed, and people could be lying to us, but I continue to think that your friend just ran away."

Lastly, I ask the question that has been tormenting me. "Do you think suicide is a serious possibility?"

The silence this time is unbroken, and I hear it as a sort of confession.

"He was fragile, Nicolas," I say. "We know that now. His father's violence . . . his parents' divorce . . . the bullying at school."

"Nobody kills himself over that," the captain says with a certainty that seems intended to turn me away from this particular path of inquiry.

I repeat this sentence in my head, slowly. And then, in a quiet voice, I ask: "Do you know why people kill themselves?"

When I hang up, I think: There were six of us—five boys and a girl—and we were carefree, laughing, happy, in a summer where anything seemed possible. Why did one of us have to disappear?

Days passed.

I continued to get up late, to feel the cold tiles of the kitchen floor under my bare feet as I ate breakfast, to help Virginie bury dead toads in the garden, to walk along the hollyhock-lined paths to the market, to kiss Christian's cheeks outside his van and smell his sour wine breath, to meet up with my parents at L'Escale, to watch my father read his newspaper while wondering if I would do that one day, just like him. I continued to go to the beach every afternoon at the hottest time of day, sometimes to lie on a towel or dive into the waves, sometimes simply to watch people from behind my sunglasses. I continued to give Anne-Marie a hand at the French fry stall now and then, and to play pinball at L'Ambiance—I could play there for hours on end without stopping. I continued to drink cans of beer and go to sleep late, in my makeshift bed next to François's. But it was not like before.

I thought about Nicolas. Once, I even felt sure I recognized him on a street corner. That skinny body, that telltale gait. I ran after him. It wasn't him, of course. It was just a mirage, a hallucination conjured by my imagination, by my hope.

191

(I didn't know then that this would happen to me again and again during the years that followed. I would learn that we never completely give up on a hope. I would learn that our rememberings make us see ghosts, write books.)

And then came the moment when we stopped believing he had run away. It would have been too cruel of Nicolas to hide in silence for that long, to let people suffer such torture without seeking to bring it to an end, one way or another. Besides, running away is a way of distancing yourself, not of burying yourself. He could easily have sent a message indirectly to one or several of us; there was no need for this absolute silence. You might run away on a sudden impulse. But once you calm down, you realize what you've done. And you are rapidly brought back to the demands of reality: you need to eat, drink, find somewhere to sleep. A runaway, ultimately, is almost always found. A runaway is human, not a ghost: he is visible, he leaves tracks, he lowers his guard, he makes mistakes.

Then came the moment when we were left with a choice of only the cruelest possibilities.

The moment when, almost despite ourselves, despite refusing to do this for so long, we imperceptibly began talking about him in the past tense.

We also understood that we had nobody with whom we could share this story, beyond the three of us: François, Christophe, and me, the only ones still on the island that summer.

Just after August 15, my parents and I took the ferry again

and we went home. My mother's annual leave was almost over, my father had to get back to his classroom, and I had to move to Rouen. Fall would soon be here.

(As I write this, an image comes to mind: Just before the ferry reached the mainland, my father came up to look for me on the gangway, sounding vaguely annoyed, to tell me I needed to come back to the car, parked down below. "Coming," I muttered, without turning to look at him. Instead of walking away, he stepped closer and said quietly: "You'll catch a cold in this wind." I think he'd sensed how upset I was, and this was his way of showing tenderness.)

One day, a few weeks later, I thought: Well, people have the *right to disappear*, don't they? The right to vanish into thin air, to elude others, to escape them without warning, without explanation, as if by magic. Those who disappear, they have their reasons. These reasons may be indecipherable to anyone else, but they should be respected, not questioned. Being able to disappear was a basic freedom, in other words.

Thinking about the three of us, I wondered: perhaps we had to go through this kind of ordeal to grow up, to become adults? Because we clearly emerged different people after this unexpected tragedy. Transformed by the insoluble mystery, we would never be the same afterward. We had lost our sweet naivety. From now on, things would be serious.

*　　*　　*

Finally, I thought: Sometimes someone has to disappear to remind us of the value of life, to make us understand how fragile and precious it is. By leaving, perhaps Nicolas taught us a lesson. A cruel and magnificent lesson.

EPILOGUE

Christophe gave up being a fisherman on his thirtieth birthday. He opened a small restaurant at Bois-Plage. You have to walk through a pine forest to reach it. In July and August, it's always packed. You should book in advance if you want to get a table there. François's father died of cancer at the age of fifty-five, and François took over his business. He still works the butcher van at the La Noue market every morning without fail. Times have changed, but his customers have remained faithful. Alice became a movie producer, and has been responsible for several award-winning art films. Marc worked as an engineer in Paris before moving to the United States, where he met his future husband, a brilliant lawyer. They have two children together.

As for me, I started writing books.

We never found out what happened to Nicolas Tardieu. He didn't reappear, and his body was never discovered. We will never know what actually happened during the night of July 19, 1985.

This is probably why his memory has haunted me through all these years. An unsolved mystery can easily become an obsession.

I suppose he must be dead. Sometimes, though, I find myself thinking that this melancholy boy, the one who smoked a Marlboro while leaning against a wall on a long-lost summer day, is alive and well somewhere. And that one bright sunlit morning he'll smile at us again—the five of us, miraculously reunited—and, after tossing his cigarette stub onto the sidewalk, he'll walk toward us, as if nothing had happened.

PHILIPPE BESSON is a prizewinning author, screenwriter, and playwright. His first novel, *In the Absence of Men*, was awarded the Emmanuel-Roblès Prize in 2001, and he is also the author of *Lie with Me*, a number one French bestseller. His novels have been translated into twenty different languages.

SAM TAYLOR is an award-winning literary translator and novelist. He has translated over seventy books from French, including works by Laurent Binet, Leïla Slimani, David Diop, and Marcel Proust. Born in England, Sam was a journalist at *The Observer* (London) before moving to France. He now lives in the United States with his family.